all I want is everything

^a gossip girl _{novel}

Gossip Girl novels by Cecily von Ziegesar:

Gossip Girl
You Know You Love Me
All I Want is Everything

all I want is everything
a gossip girl
novel

by

Cecily von Ziegesar

LITTLE, BROWN AND COMPANY

New York ❧ An AOL Time Warner Company

First Edition

The characters and events in this book are fictitious. Any similarity to real persons, living or dead, is coincidental and not intended by the author.

 Produced by 17th Street Productions,
an Alloy company
151 West 26th Street, New York, NY 10001

ISBN 0-316-91212-3

CIP data is available

10 9 8 7 6 5 4 3 2 1
CWO
Printed in the United States of America

all I want is everything

I wanna, I wanna, I gotta be adored.
　　　　　　　　　　　　—The Stone Roses

 gossipgirl.net

Disclaimer: All the real names of places, people, and events have been altered or abbreviated to protect the innocent. Namely, me.

hey people!

Christmastime in New York City really is magical, especially uptown. The air smells like falling snow and burning logs and Christmas cookies baking. From up in our penthouses, Central Park looks like a silvery wonderland, Park Avenue is a parade of Christmas lights, and the size of the tree in Rockefeller Center seems to promise that this is going to be the most amazing Christmas ever—although most of us will be drinking too much champagne to notice. Along Fifth Avenue, the department store windows are all dressed up for the holidays, and the girls out shopping are wearing those gorgeous sky blue cashmere Marc Jacobs coats they bought in October and couldn't wait to wear. And at night, everyone is out having fun, fun, *fun*. Forget studying for midterms; forget those last-minute college applications; forget helping your mom buy presents for the maids, the cooks, the drivers, and the laundry ladies. Grab your black satin Prada wrap dress, your Christian Louboutin four-inch stilettos with the clear Perspex heels, your orange Hermès Birkin bag, and the cutest boy you know and come out with me!

Sightings

D and **V** with their lips locked down by the Seventy-ninth Street boat basin. It's kind of tragic how long it took them to realize they liked each other. **N** buying red roses for **J**—and you didn't think he had a sweet bone in his gorgeous stoner body. **B** and **S** heading into **Bendel's** to pick up their dresses for the **Black-and-White Ball** tonight. I hear **Flow**—former model and gorgeous lead singer and guitar player, whose band, **45**, just won the **MTV Music Award** for best album for their debut album, **Komunik8**—is going to do the honor of announcing how much money was raised. The ball is a benefit for **Be Kind**, an animal rights group for which Flow is a spokesperson. But who cares about that? We all know we're only going so we can catch a glimpse of his perfect face. See you there!

Are they really friends again?

It's true: **S** and **B** have decided to kiss and make up, and it's about time. I mean, how long can you actually stay mad at someone you took baths with in grade school? **B** may not be as blond or as tall or as "experienced" as **S**, but that doesn't mean she has to hate her. And **S** will never be as devious or as self-absorbed as **B**, but that doesn't mean she has to fear her. Instead, the two girls have decided to put aside their differences and be pleasant to each other, at least for the time being. The question is, now that they're back together, what kind of crazy shenanigans are they going to get up to?

Believe me, I'll be the first to find out, and you'll be the second. It's not like I'm good at keeping secrets.

You know you love me,

gossip girl

the belles of the ball

"If she was, like, six inches taller, he could rest his chin in her cleavage," Blair Waldorf observed as she watched her ex-boyfriend, Nate Archibald, dancing with Jennifer Humphrey, the short and extremely buxom ninth grader for whom Nate had unexplainably ditched Blair only a few weeks ago. "But then again, he might have trouble breathing."

Luckily, Blair had skipped dinner that night; otherwise she would have headed straight for the ladies' room to vomit in disgust.

Serena van der Woodsen, Blair's oldest and newest best friend, shook her pale blond head in response. "I don't get it," she said. "I have nothing against Jenny, but I always thought you and Nate were, like, the *perfect* couple. You were totally *destined* to spend the rest of your lives together."

It was a strange thing for Serena to say. After all, she and Nate had lost their virginity together behind Blair's back the summer after tenth grade. If any two people were destined for each other, you'd have thought it would have been them. But as with every relationship Serena had ever had, her little fling with Nate had been just a spur-of-the-moment affair. Blair and Nate were the *real thing*. And they had always been such a reliable fixture—like the doorman in the lobby of Serena's Fifth Avenue apartment building—that it was impossible to fathom what the future might be like without them as a couple. Through them Serena sampled what it would be like to be a part of a committed relationship, and it was a little scary to see how badly things had turned out.

Blair gulped her glass of Cristal champagne thirstily. The two girls were sitting alone at a big, round table draped in white muslin and black taffeta in the opulent ballroom at the St. Claire Hotel, where the annual December Black-and-White Ball was in full swing. Girls in long, strappy black dresses by Versace and Dolce & Gabbana with white feathers in their hair were dancing with boys in crisp black-and-white Tom Ford for Gucci tuxedos, and a gigantic ball made of black and white roses hung from the ceiling. Blair was having major déjà vu.

Her mother had been married only a month ago to a loud, sweaty, overweight loser named Cyrus Rose, and the wedding reception had taken place in that very same room. The wedding had also taken place on Blair's seventeenth birthday, the day she'd planned to go all the way with Nate. She'd spent hours grooming herself and had played out every moment of how it was going to be over and over in her head. But then she'd stumbled upon Nate making out with that little girl in the hotel lobby and realized that in the end, it didn't matter how hot she looked in her espresso-colored Chloé maid of honor dress, or how dramatic her hair was, or how high her pewter Manolo Blahnik stilettos were. Nate was too busy groping that fuzzy-headed fourteen-year-old's balloon breasts to even notice.

It had been by far the worst birthday Blair had ever had. But she wasn't about to dwell on it. She wasn't like that.

Yeah, right.

"I don't believe in destiny anymore," she told Serena, plonking her crystal champagne flute down on the table and nearly breaking its stem. She ran her fingers through her long, dark brown hair, which had been trimmed earlier that day by Antoine, her new favorite hairdresser at the Elizabeth Arden Red Door Salon.

Serena laughed and rolled her dark blue eyes. "Then how come you're always saying Yale is your destiny?"

"That's different," Blair insisted.

Blair's father had gone to Yale, and Blair had always dreamed of going there, too. She was at the top of her class at Constance Billard and had extracurriculars coming out of her ass, so applying early admission had seemed like an obvious choice. But during her interview, she'd cracked under pressure and become Blair, Drama Queen of the Silver Screen. She'd told her interviewer a heart-wrenching sob story about how her mother had divorced her gay father and was about to marry a man she barely knew, and how she couldn't wait to go to college so she could start a whole new life. And then she'd kissed her interviewer—actually stood on her tippytoes and kissed him on his hollow, stubbly cheek!

Blair was always imagining herself as the heroine of some black-and-white fifties movie, in the style of Audrey Hepburn, her idol. This time it had been her downfall. Now she'd been forced to apply to Yale regular admission along with everyone else, and she'd even had to ask her father to donate a Yale study abroad program in France to help give her a leg up. But her chances of getting in were still slim at best.

Blair reached for the bottle of Cristal sitting in its silver cooler in the middle of the large, round table and filled her glass. "Destiny is for losers," she said. "It's just a lame excuse for letting things happen to you instead of *making* them happen."

If only she knew exactly how to make the things she wanted to happen *happen* without fucking them up completely.

Serena's attention span was shorter than that of a newborn puppy, and she had already drunk way too much wine to have such a serious conversation. "Let's not talk about the future for once, okay?" she said. She lit a cigarette and blew smoke into the air above Blair's head. "You know, that blond kid Aaron's talking to has been totally staring at you for the last ten minutes." She covered her mouth with her long, slender fingers and giggled. "Oops. Here they come."

Blair turned around to find her dreadlocked vegan stepbrother, Aaron Rose, and an extremely tall boy with spiky blond hair and light brown eyes, wearing a fabulously tailored Armani tux, walking over to their table. The boy drummed his long fingers nervously against his superlong legs and looked down at his shiny black Christian Dior dress shoes, as if he was worried about tripping over them or something. Behind the two boys, the dance floor was heaving with gorgeous, gorgeously dressed girls and adorably handsome boys, their arms wound around each other's necks, swaying to a Beck song.

"Say something nice to Blair," Serena told Aaron. "She's stressing about the future."

Blair rolled her eyes. "Who isn't?"

Aaron's thin red lips curled down in an apologetic frown. He, Blair, and Serena had come to the ball together, and as soon as they'd arrived, Aaron had left the two girls to drink and smoke cigarettes while he went and found his friends. But Blair had been kind of wound-up and emotional lately, what with their parents' wedding and her lousy Yale interview and everything. She needed all the moral support she could get. "Sorry. I haven't been a very good date. Wanna dance or something?"

Blair ignored him. Did she look like she felt like dancing? She glanced at Aaron's tall, blond friend. "Who are you?"

The blond boy grinned. His teeth were even whiter than his shirt. "I'm Miles. Miles Ingram."

Son of Danny Ingram, the famous restaurant and night-club owner, proprietor of such hot spots as Gorgon in New York and Trixie in LA, to name just a few.

"He's in my class at Bronxdale," Aaron added. "We're starting a band. Miles plays the drums."

Blair sipped her champagne, waiting for them to say something that wasn't completely boring.

Miles grinned at Blair and drummed his fingers on the back of an empty chair. "You're much prettier than I thought," he said.

He was cute, but the drumming fingers thing could get seriously annoying.

Blair didn't smile back. She picked up her drink. Aaron had probably told Miles she was a total witch, and he'd expected her to have warts on her nose and a broom up her ass.

Not exactly. Aaron just didn't like to talk about his new stepsister because he wanted to keep her all to himself. But don't get your fishnets in a twist—we'll get to that later.

Aaron pushed his dreadlocks behind his ears. "And this is Serena," he told Miles.

Miles gave Serena's perfectly chiseled face, deep blue eyes, long, lithe body, and fantastic black Gucci dress the once-over. He let his eyes linger on her a moment—it was hard not to—before turning back to Aaron. "It's weird. You didn't say anything about Blair being so beautiful."

Aaron shrugged and looked uncomfortable. "Sorry."

Blair and Serena lit new cigarettes, still waiting for some-thing crazy to happen. Considering the point Blair had just made about destiny, it was up to them to *make* it happen.

Aaron cleared his throat. "Sure you don't want to dance?" he asked Blair again.

Blair noticed that he wasn't wearing a bow tie and that his tuxedo shirt was untucked and unbuttoned at the throat. Apparently he was making a statement. She took a long drag on her cigarette and blew smoke in his face. "No, thanks."

The Beck song ended, and people crowded back to their tables to fill up on booze.

"My feet are dying!" Kati Farkas whined, flinging herself down on a chair opposite Blair and whipping off her heels.

"Mine are already dead," Isabel Coates chimed in, sinking into the chair next to her.

For the past two years, while Serena had been away at Hanover Academy in New Hampshire, Isabel and Kati had been glued to Blair's side. They bought makeup at Sephora together, they drank cappuccinos at Le Canard together, and yes, they even went to the bathroom together. Blair ruled the social scene, so when they were with her they felt almost famous, getting red-carpet treatment everywhere. But just before Columbus Day, Serena had gotten kicked out of boarding school and reappeared in the city to steal Blair away from them, and Kati and Isabel had gone back to being plain old Kati and Isabel again.

"How come you guys aren't dancing?" asked Kati.

Blair shrugged. "I'm not in the mood."

Isabel sighed. "All we have to do is make it through midterms next week," she said, mistaking the note of boredom in Blair's voice for fatigue. "And then we get to go away for Christmas."

"You guys are so lucky you're going someplace hot," Kati added. "I have to go stupid skiing in stupid Aspen, *again*."

"Well, that's not as bad my boring country house in Connecticut," replied Isabel.

"It's going to be awesome," Serena gushed with an excited smile.

Kati and Isabel glared at her.

Blair and Serena were going to St. Bart's together for Christmas break. Blair's mom and Aaron's dad had spent their honeymoon cruising in the Caribbean and had arranged to meet Blair, Aaron, and Blair's little brother, Tyler, for the holidays at the exclusive Isle de la Paix resort in St. Barts. They were each allowed to bring a friend if they wanted, so after making up in the bathroom during her mother's wedding reception, Blair had asked Serena.

Of course they'd be back in the city for New Year's. No self-respecting party girl spends New Year's away with her parents after the age of twelve.

"It's going to kick ass," Blair agreed with a smug smile. She could picture herself perfectly, slick with tanning oil, in her new Missoni bikini on a pristine white-sand beach, her face masked by enormous Chanel sunglasses, while hot guys in surf shorts brought her exotic drinks in coconut shells. She was going to forget about Yale and Nate and her mother and Cyrus and just bake herself brown as café au lait under the hot island sun. Of course she knew Kati and Isabel were totally jealous that she hadn't asked either one of them to come to St. Barts with her, but to be honest, she didn't give a rat's squiggly ass.

Only one more week to go.

Chuck Bass came up behind Blair and put his big, warm hands on her bare, tennis-toned shoulders. "I just saw Nate and that little girl from Constance feeling each other up in the corner," he announced, as if everyone wanted to know.

Chuck was handsome in a dark, after-shave commercial sort of way. He was also the horniest boy in all of New York City. He had tried to molest Serena when she was passed out drunk in his family's Tribeca Star Hotel suite in October, and he had almost gotten little Jenny Humphrey to take her dress off for him in the ladies' room at the *Kiss on the Lips* party that same week. Chuck was the worst sort of slimeball, but they all still put up with him, because he was one of them: He went to a small, private all-boys' school; in grade school he'd gone to dancing school at Arthur Murray and tennis lessons at Asphalt Green and sung in the church of the beachfront hotel in the South of France. He got invited to the best parties and the most exclusive private sales, just like they all did, and he was born to live the high life, just like they all were. Even when he got rejected, Chuck still came back for more. He was ruthlessly unflappable.

Blair tried to shrug his hands away. "So?"

Chuck kept his hands where they were. "Nate never got you to give it up, did he?" He began massaging her shoulders. "I was thinking maybe I should be the one to do the honors."

Blair's whole body stiffened. Until that moment, she'd never had much of a problem with Chuck, but now she understood why Serena hated his guts. She pushed her chair back, wrenching her shoulders away from his hands, and stood up. "I have to pee," she announced to the table, ignoring Chuck entirely. "Then let's get out of here. We can have a party back at my house or something."

Aaron stood up and took a step toward her, tucking his dreadlocks behind his ears self-consciously. "Are you okay?" he asked, sounding concerned.

At that moment, his whole Mr. Sensitive act annoyed Blair almost as much as Chuck's sliminess.

"I'm fine."

She turned and marched across the room as best as she could wearing four-inch Christian Louboutin Perspex stilettos and a supertight black Gucci dress, keeping her eyes straight ahead of her to avoid the sight of Nate with that little Ginny girl, or whatever the hell her name was.

People were gathering on the dance floor, murmuring excitedly. It looked like Flow—the hottest lead singer in music—was about to make his appearance. But Blair didn't care. She didn't go crazy over famous people, like most girls. She didn't need to: She was the constant star of the feature film playing in her head, the most famous person she knew.

rock star hottie turns the beat around

Jenny had been in a sort of blissed-out trance all evening. Before escorting her to the Black-and-White Ball, Nate had dressed up in a new Donna Karan tuxedo, picked her up in a cab, taken her out for sushi and too much sake at Bond, and given her a little turquoise star-shaped Jade Jagger pendant. His green eyes sparkled in the candlelight, and his golden brown hair was so perfectly tousled, Jenny kept taking mental Polaroids so she could paint a brand-new portrait of him in the morning to add to her collection.

The best part was that after they'd arrived at the ball, Nate hadn't dragged her around to talk to people she didn't know. Even Nate's boisterous best friends, Jeremy Scott Tompkinson, Anthony Avuldsen, and Charlie Dern, had left them alone. Tonight Nate was all hers, happy to just hold her as they kissed quietly in the corner.

"You know that painting *The Kiss*, by Gustav Klimt?" Jenny gushed, as she looked up at Nate's adorable face.

Nate frowned. "Not really."

"Yes, you do. It's totally famous. Anyway, that's what this reminds me of."

He shrugged and looked up at the stage. "I think that dude from 45 is about to come out and say something."

Jenny leaned her back against the wall. Before Nate, she would have wet her pants with excitement about seeing a celebrity like Flow, but now all she wanted was to keep kissing Nate.

"So?" She giggled and dabbed at her mouth with the back of her hand, careful not to smudge her pink MAC lip gloss. "That was nice," she added quietly.

"What?" Nate asked, glancing distractedly around the room.

"I've never kissed for that long before," Jenny admitted.

Nate turned back to her and smiled. He'd smoked a joint on the way to pick her up and was still feeling it. He liked the dress Jennifer was wearing. It was long and black, cut low in the front and back, with a dramatic white ruffle that flapped around her tiny ankles.

Jenny had bought the dress at Century 21, a discount designer store frequented by bargain hunters and desperately clueless people who will buy anything with a designer label in it, even if it's obviously imperfect or just a designer's really bad idea that wouldn't sell anywhere, except at Century 21.

It would take exactly four months' worth of allowance to pay her father back for the dress, but Nate didn't have to know that. He thought she looked like a tiny black-and-white angel. An angel with the best set of bazongas he had ever seen. He reached out and rubbed his hands up and down her pale, baby-soft arms. She felt nice, too, nice and warm, like freshly baked bread at a five-star restaurant.

The DJ started to play 45's hit song, "Korrupt Me," and then Flow swaggered onto the dance floor out of nowhere, wearing a tuxedo jacket over a red T-shirt that said BE KIND in white capital letters, and grinning like someone who knows he's one of the hottest guys in the entire world. Flow was the son of a Danish lingerie model and a Jamaican coffee mogul, and looked like a tan, blue-eyed version of Jim Morrison from the classic sixties band The Doors. He stepped behind a glass podium, the music stopped, and everyone whooped and clapped. Jenny slid her small hand into Nate's bigger one and gave it a squeeze as they stepped out of the corner to watch.

"I just want to give a shout out to all of you for dressing up and coming out tonight to raise money for . . ." Flow opened his tuxedo jacket and pointed to his T-shirt, and some of the perky, enthusiastic guests at the ball who weren't ashamed to sound like assholes shouted, *"Be Kind!"*

At that same moment, Blair pushed open the ladies' room door to find Nate and Jenny standing directly in her path, holding hands. Jenny was wearing a loud grandma-style dress of dubious design that was way too big on the bottom and way too small on top. She and Nate looked like tacky kids from the suburbs out on their prom night.

Blair adjusted the straps of her dress and smacked her ruby-red lacquered lips together. The sooner she got out of there, the better. But she couldn't just slink away like some poor ditched ex-girlfriend. She had way more fucking pride than that.

Way, *way* more.

"I'd also like to thank the organizing committee for the ball, chaired by Blair Waldorf and Serena van der Woodsen," Flow continued, reading from the little cue card in his hand. "Hey, why don't you two girls come up here and help me announce how much money you raised?"

Everyone craned their heads to look for Serena and Blair.

In her typical exuberant fashion, Serena let out a loud whooping sound and glided effortlessly across the dance floor and up to the podium with her pale hair flying. Flow took a step back, struck dumb by her loveliness, and Serena leaned into the microphone. "Come on, Blair," she cried, looking around the crowded room. "Get up here!"

Blair could feel people staring at her. She attempted a smile and left her post by the bathroom door, walking directly in front of Nate's and Jenny's noses as she made her way to the front of the room.

Nate's mouth opened as Blair swished by. She looked taller than he remembered, and her ass was more defined. Her long hair gleamed, and her skin had a pearly sheen that made him want to touch it. She looked *hot.* No, she looked better than hot. Suddenly he felt confused. He wanted to grab Blair's arm and say, "Come back here. I made a mistake." But then Jenny squeezed his hand, and he looked down into her soulful brown eyes and deeply plunging cleavage and instantly forgot about Blair again.

Nate was like the dumbest Labrador retriever. If you dangled a stick in front of him, he just had to have it, but if you threw a tennis ball, he forgot all about the stick and went after the ball.

Blair joined them at the podium and Flow handed Serena a piece of paper, grinning from ear to ear because the two chairs of the ball had turned out to be so gorgeous.

"Okay," Serena said, reading from the piece of paper. "So we raised eight hundred thousand four hundred dollars. All proceeds will go to Be Kind, the new international animal rescue fund." She showed off the famous smile that had been captured in so many photographs for the society and gossip pages and nudged Blair in the arm.

Blair had chaired hundreds of these things. She knew the drill.

She leaned into the microphone. "Thank you for coming!" she shouted, smiling her best do-gooder smile. "And don't forget your Coach gift bag—that's the best part!"

The music started up again, louder than before, and everyone went back to boozing and dancing. Flow bent his head toward Serena and whispered something in her ear. His breath was warm and tickled her ear. He smelled like new leather.

Serena giggled. "Wait one sec, okay?"

Flow nodded as Serena grabbed Blair's arm and stepped away from the podium, dragging Blair with her back to their table. "He wants me to meet him outside so we can go for a ride in his limo. Quick, get your coat. You're coming, too."

Blair frowned. She really wasn't the third-wheel type, thank you very much. "I don't think so."

Serena pretended she didn't hear her. She wasn't going to let Blair poop all over her party.

Kati, Isabel, Chuck, Aaron, and Miles were still sitting at the table, drinking shots of Stoli that Chuck had snuck in with him in a silver monogrammed flask. "Come on," Serena told them gleefully. "Everybody outside! We're moving the party to Flow's limo!"

Blair fished her coat-check ticket out of her not exactly cruelty-free mink-and-armadillo-skin Fendi baguette purse. Sometimes Serena's enthusiasm verged on annoying. But it wasn't like she'd been having the time of her life at the ball.

She liked the idea of being all dressed up and riding around town watching the world go by through smoky limousine windows. It was so Audrey in *Breakfast at Tiffany's*.

And maybe a ride in Flow's limo would be just the thing to magically transform her life from a series of disasters to a series of dreams come true.

Or maybe not.

Nate was getting kind of bored of just kissing Jenny. He hadn't had much to drink, and he really needed another joint.

"Want to go for a walk or something?" he asked.

Jenny smiled up at him. His eyelashes looked like they'd been dipped in gold, just like his hair. The only thing that would make tonight even more perfect than it already was would be if Nate told her, "I love you." And hopefully that was exactly what he was about to do. "Sure," she replied eagerly.

They retrieved their coats, and Nate held the door open for her as they left the bustling hotel.

A massive black limo with smoky black windows was parked outside. Nate and Jenny walked down the marble steps to the sidewalk, and Nate let go of her hand to discreetly light a joint. Jenny fiddled with her black suede gloves, disappointed. If Nate was going to say, "I love you," she didn't want him to be baked when he did it.

All of a sudden, the back window of the limo rolled down and Serena's beautiful blond head appeared.

"Hey, you guys!" she said to Nate and Jenny. "Come on! We're having a party! Get in! Get in!"

As usual, Serena was acting on impulse. It didn't even occur to her that they were the last fucking people on earth Blair wanted to see.

Jenny had always pretty much worshipped Serena, and riding around with her and whoever else was in the car sounded exciting and decadent. More exciting than walking around in the freezing cold while Nate got high. She touched Nate's arm. "Can we?"

Nate shrugged. He was up for anything, as long as he could bring his joint with him. "Sure," he said. "Why not?"

The door swung open, and Jenny giggled excitedly as she clambered over the mass of fishnet-clad legs and tuxedoed knees and wriggled into a tiny spot near the window next to a girl wearing the most amazing and expensive-looking shoes she had ever seen. A girl who happened to be Nate's ex-girlfriend, Blair Waldorf.

Jenny's face turned tomato red, and she immediately turned her head the other way, only to make direct eye contact with a leering Chuck Bass, the asshole who had tried to smother her in a bathroom stall at the *Kiss on the Lips* party in October.

See what happens when you dive into a limo without checking to see who's in it first?

d might save himself for marriage

Daniel Humphrey bit Vanessa Abrams's pinky nail off and spat it onto the brown shag rug on his bedroom floor. The nail was much longer than the others, and he was tired of the way she was always accidentally scratching him with it.

"Hey, that was my guitar nail," Vanessa protested, wrestling her hand away from him and examining the damage.

Dan laughed, his pale face scrunching up beneath his shaggy brown hair. He rarely got a haircut, but the overgrown look suited his disheveled, overcaffeinated poet image. "Like you play guitar."

Vanessa shrugged and rubbed the top of her dark, close-shaven head with a pale knuckle. She had enormous brown eyes, pale skin, and thin red lips and might even have been pretty if she stopped shaving her head. But Vanessa wasn't into prettiness; she preferred the darker sides of things, their ugly underbellies.

"How do you know?" she said. "During the day I hang out with you, but at night, I rock."

"You don't even like loud music," Dan scoffed. He pushed her down on the bed and started to tickle her under the arms. "Your favorite CD is a recording of a thunderstorm."

"Stop!" Vanessa screeched, thrashing her arms and legs and snorting hysterically. "Daniel Randolph Humphrey, you stop it right now!"

Aw, aren't they cute?

Dan stopped tickling her and sat up. "You said the *R* word."

Vanessa pulled her black turtleneck shirt down where it had ridden up over her pale, slightly chubby stomach. "Randolph, Randolph, Randolph. Who gives their kid a middle name like Randolph, anyway? It sounds like the name of a condom or a porn star or something. Randolph the Lubricator!" she howled.

Dan got very quiet all of a sudden, frowning as he poked his finger into a cigarette burn in the ancient green wool army surplus blanket on his bed.

Vanessa sat up. "I'm sorry. I promised I wouldn't make fun of your middle name and now here I am, laughing at it like a jackass."

But that wasn't what was bothering Dan.

"Clark is what, like, twenty-two?" he asked.

Vanessa's brown eyes got even bigger. Clark was the older bartender she'd been seeing before Dan had finally gotten with the program and realized that he and Vanessa should be more than friends. "Yeah, so?"

"And he's a bartender. Kind of a stud?"

"I guess." She still couldn't see what he was getting at.

Dan scooted back on his bed and lit his millionth Camel of the day. He inhaled deeply and blew a blue-gray stream of smoke into the air above Vanessa's head. She could tell he was trying to look composed, but his eyes were nervous.

"So were you guys . . . um . . . having sex, or what?"

Vanessa tried to suppress her smile. So that was what this was about. She considered her answer. "Kind of."

"Like, you kind of were, or you kind of weren't?"

"Like, we did it, but not that much," Vanessa replied vaguely. She and Clark had had sex twice. The first time had been in broad daylight, and she'd felt so self-conscious about her body that she hadn't really paid that much attention to anything else. The second time she'd felt more relaxed, but still couldn't see why it was such a big deal. To her it seemed amusingly prehistoric. Like, it really was exactly the same thing all those zebras and hyenas did during mating season on those nature shows. Still, it was kind of cool to have done it already. It made her feel like she had more substance, a been-there-done-that sort of history.

"I see." Dan took another drag on his cigarette. And then another. He traced the stitching on the hem of his white, coffee-stained pillowcase. He was a virgin and Vanessa wasn't. He didn't know how he felt about that.

Actually, he did. He felt nervous, stupid, short, skinny, pale, weird, and completely inadequate. What did she have to go and have sex with some other guy for?

"Look, I know you're a virgin," Vanessa said bluntly. "But that doesn't mean you have to stay one." She raised her thick black eyebrows suggestively and grinned.

Dan looked up and grinned back, his cheeks turning an adorably embarrassed hot pink. "Really?"

Vanessa nodded and inched toward him. "Really." She put her hands on his skinny chest and pushed him down on the bed. Then she pulled the cigarette out of his hand and dunked it in the half-empty mug of stale coffee on his bedside table. "Don't worry," she said in her best husky, experienced-woman voice. "I know what I'm doing."

She kissed him softly on the mouth and then began to undress them both. First she pulled off his gray T-shirt, and then she pulled off her black one. She was wearing a black tank top underneath it. Everything Vanessa wore was black.

Dan took a deep breath and closed his eyes. This wasn't how he'd imagined it would happen. For him, sex was right up there with birth and death as one of the most intense, poetic experiences a person could have. It wasn't something you did with your girlfriend when you were bored one Saturday night before midterms. It was something you did when you had already explored each other in every other way—intellectually, spiritually, philosophically. Dan had even toyed with the idea of waiting to have sex until he was married and ready to have children. He wanted to have five children and name them after his favorite writers: Kafka, Goethe, Sartre, Camus, and Keats. Even if he didn't wait until he was married, the first time was supposed to be a process of discovery, like you were learning to talk to each other in a new language.

But Vanessa had already learned the language from some other guy.

"You have really narrow feet," she observed, kneeling on the floor as she pulled Dan's socks off.

Dan sat up and pulled his feet away from her. "Wait."

Vanessa crawled up the mattress and sat down next to him, cross-legged, in just her black tights and her black tank top. "What's wrong?"

"I don't want to do this," Dan said. He folded his skinny arms over his bare chest. His corduroys were still on, but he felt very naked. "I mean, not right now."

Vanessa reached out and poked him playfully in the arm. "I was nervous the first time, too. It's really no big deal," she said reassuringly. "Promise."

Dan swallowed and looked up at the ceiling. He kept his eyes fixed on a crack in the molding above his head. "I'd just rather wait until it's more . . . organic."

"*O*-kay," Vanessa said slowly. "But this is just sex, you know. It's not a poem."

Obviously, she didn't get it. To Dan it *was* a poem. Probably the most important poem he would ever write.

He reached for his T-shirt and pulled it on over his head. "I'd just really rather wait, that's all."

"Fine," Vanessa said, on the verge of losing her patience. Dan was always overanalyzing things, writing about them in his little black notebooks until there was nothing left to write. She loved how sensitive and romantic he was, but for once it might be nice if he forgot to think about things so much and just went with the damned flow. Still, she'd had a crush on him ever since the day they'd met and become best friends three years ago. She wasn't about to ruin things now that they were finally together.

Dan lit another cigarette. His hands were shaking like crazy.

Vanessa poked him again. "Hey, don't worry so much. I'm fine with not doing it. Okay?"

He nodded, and Vanessa grabbed his hand and pulled his arm around her shoulders. They settled back on the bed, and Dan blew smoke up into the red Chinese paper lantern overhead as he gently stroked the side of Vanessa's dark stubbly head with his thumb. He was glad he didn't have to explain himself too much. That was the nice thing about going out with his best friend. She knew him almost better than he knew himself.

They lay like that for a while, watching the smoke from his cigarette float up into the air. That was the other nice thing about going out with your best friend. You didn't always have to talk.

"As soon as break starts, I want to shoot some more film,"

Vanessa said, breaking the silence. "I'm worried my *War and Peace* film was way too dark to send to NYU."

The last film Vanessa made was adapted from a scene in Tolstoy's *War and Peace* and featured Dan as a crack-addicted Prince Andrei. Vanessa had applied early to NYU and wanted to send them one of her films instead of a written essay, since filmmaking was what she planned to major in. She couldn't wait. Only one more term at the Constance Billard School for Skinny, Uptight Girls, where (thank God) she didn't fit in at all, and she'd be free, free, free!

Dan blew out a long puff of smoke. He didn't know what Vanessa was worried about. Her films were dark, but that was what made them brilliant. There was no way NYU wouldn't take her. "If anyone has to worry, it's me," he said, his hands shaking nervously again.

"What do you mean?" Vanessa demanded. "Any school with a halfway decent writing program would kill to have you."

"Yeah, but talk about dark. My poems are really—" Dan stopped. His poems were *personal*, that was what they were. And it seemed sort of strange to send a whole slew of them off to some random admissions person at Columbia or Brown or Vassar, like he was baring his soul to a complete stranger who might not have even read the works of Goethe, Sartre, or Camus and wouldn't understand his oblique references to their work.

"You know, you might even think about trying to get some of your stuff published," Vanessa suggested. "That would really get the college admissions people all worked up about you."

Dan stubbed out his cigarette butt in an empty Coke can. "Yeah, right," he said. He liked to write, but no way was he ready to send stuff out to be published. He hadn't even found his voice yet. He knew that. Every new poem he wrote sounded different from the old ones.

Vanessa sat up again. "What? I'm serious. You should do it."

Dan slumped down further under the covers. "Whatever," he mumbled halfheartedly. He wasn't ready for sex, and he wasn't ready to be published. Now he felt even more inadequate.

Vanessa knew when it was time to back off. She took a deep breath and channeled her inner pussycat, the one who only got up from her warm spot on the radiator when Dan needed a rough kiss on his cute little face.

She slid under the covers and kissed his chin. "One more week and we can spend all of break like this," she murmured.

Unlike most of their classmates at Constance Billard and Riverside Prep, neither Vanessa nor Dan would be going anywhere glamorous for break. Vanessa lived with her older bass guitar player sister, Ruby, in an apartment in the Williamsburg section of Brooklyn. Their parents were avant-garde artists who lived in Vermont and always spent Christmas on tour with their performance-art troupe. Dan and his sister, Jenny, lived with their father, Rufus, a Communist writer and editor of lesser-known Beat poets, who didn't believe in Christmas or Hanukkah, or any other holiday, for that matter.

"Dad's cooking his once-a-year lasagna dinner on Friday," Dan said and ran his hands along Vanessa's back, allowing himself to relax again. He loved how smooth and solid her back felt, not all ribby, like his own. "You're coming, right?"

She shrugged. "Sure. But tell your dad I'm not going to pig out like I did last year. That's another thing I'm doing over break. I'm going to lose five pounds."

Dan kept stroking her back. "Why?" he asked. Vanessa didn't need to go on a diet. Her body was just the way he'd described it in one of his poems: like water.

"Because my clothes will fit better if I do." Vanessa wasn't interested in being emaciated, like most of her classmates, but she didn't like it when she had to suck in her stomach to button her pants.

"Well, I like you how you are," Dan said, nuzzling his nose into her ear.

Vanessa turned her head toward him, and their lips met in a long, sweet kiss. As they kissed, she couldn't help but think that sex with Dan might be a whole lot more meaningful than it had been with Clark. If only Dan were ready.

"I love you," he whispered, opening his intense brown eyes.

"I love you, too," she whispered, closing hers. Briefly she considered asking him again if he wanted to try having sex, but she didn't want to ruin the moment. She'd just have to wait until he was ready, although with Dan that might mean waiting until they were married or something.

Yawn. As if they didn't act like they were already.

j regrets joining the party

In the backseat of Flow's limo, Blair found herself wedged between that big-boobed Jenny Humphrey and Aaron's gangly, spiky-haired drummer friend, Miles. Across from them, Serena was sitting on Flow's lap—"to make room for everyone else," she claimed—and Nate was huddled by the window, getting high. He had also rolled joints for Kati, Isabel, and Chuck, who were even more annoying when they were baked than when they were drunk. Aaron was sitting cross-legged on the floor between the two backseats, smoking one of his herbal cigarettes and playing with the limo's PlayStation 2.

"What's your real name, anyway?" Serena asked Flow, even though she already knew from watching MTV that his name was Julian Prospere. It was actually a whole lot better name than Flow, but she wasn't about to say that.

He grinned the famous shy-boy grin captured on the covers of *Spin*, *Rolling Stone*, *Entertainment Weekly*, and *Interview* and shook his head. "Not telling."

"Well, you're not as good-looking in person," she said, turning her head away from him with a wicked little smile. She was lying, of course. He was at least ten times *better*-looking than in his photographs, if that was even possible.

Serena knew she was being ridiculously flirtatious, but she loved the way Flow's dark brown hair curled around his temples, his golden bronze skin, and how long and delicate looking his fingers were. Why not flirt with him? It was only a one-night thing. Tomorrow Flow would go back to LA or wherever he lived, and she would finally start studying for midterms. All she wanted was to have a little fun.

All Serena *ever* wanted was to have a little fun.

Flow winced, pretending to be ashamed of his godlike appearance. "Sorry. I guess I'm not as tall, either."

He bent down and swung open the little Sub-Zero fridge beneath his seat. "Hey, we got beverages here. Anybody thirsty?"

"Yes, please," Blair answered immediately. Getting good and drunk was the only way to tolerate any of this.

"Um, I'll try some," Jenny ventured timidly. The limo lurched over a manhole, and her boobs bounced mercilessly. She glanced at Nate to see if he'd noticed, but he was looking out the window with that spaced-out look he got when he was extremely stoned.

Miles helped Flow fill ten crystal champagne flutes. He handed one to Blair. "Cheers," he said, clinking his against hers.

Blair took the glass and, since she wasn't sitting next to the window and had nothing else to look at, considered Miles's face. He had round, golden brown eyes, sort of like Mookie's, Aaron's dog. His pert little ski-jump nose was dusted with tiny freckles, and his white-blond hair stuck straight up. Judging from the way the veins stuck out from his long neck, he probably worked out or played basketball or something. All in all, he looked sort of like a cartoon character with an athlete's body. But since she had nothing better to do and he was clearly hot for her, Blair thought it might be mildly entertaining to flirt with him.

She put her hand on his leg. "Thanks," she said, taking a sip of her champagne.

Miles smiled as though he thought this was the beginning of a beautiful friendship.

Flow couldn't stop drooling over Serena. "You really are the most beautiful girl I've seen in a while," he murmured in her ear. "Maybe ever. I can't believe you're not a model or an actress or anything."

Serena dipped her fingers in her champagne glass and then put them in her mouth. Considering how famous he was, she'd thought Flow would be all cocky and smooth-talking, but he was surprisingly earnest. If he hadn't been a gorgeous rock star, this might have been a total turn-off, but he *was* a gorgeous rock star, so she decided to overlook it.

"Nope," she said. "I'm just me."

In fact, pictures of Serena were constantly appearing in society columns and magazines; she just didn't get paid for them—she didn't need to.

Flow kept on staring at her.

Serena giggled. "Stop it."

"Ooh, baby," Chuck said obnoxiously, sucking on his joint. "Somebody is getting some tonight!" He closed his eyes. It looked like he was about to pass out.

"I'm starving," Kati said. She opened the ashtray in the limo door and then closed it again. "Don't you have any food?"

"I feel all . . . *prickly*," Isabel declared with her eyes bugging out of her head.

Aaron glanced up from the floor to find Blair sitting very close to Miles, her hand resting carelessly on his knee. Without finishing the game, he switched off the PlayStation 2 and stood up, squeezing to fit between them on the seat.

"Ow," Blair whined as his skinny butt rammed her hip.

"Well, shove over, then," Aaron said. "Hey, where are we going, anyway?" he asked Flow.

Flow ran his long musician's fingers through Serena's endless blond hair and shrugged. "Downtown. Maybe stop at a club."

Jenny clutched her champagne flute and squirmed in her seat. It was fine for all of them to go to a club. They looked older than they were, and probably all had fake IDs. Despite her chest, Jenny still looked about ten years old. She even got carded at Blockbuster renting R-rated videos! The last thing she wanted was to watch everyone glide through the doors of a cool club while the bouncer kindly asked her if it wasn't way past her bedtime. She should have just gone on a walk with Nate. She always had a much better time when they were alone together than when they were with other people.

"Nate?" she said, leaning forward and taking his hand. "I should probably go home soon." It was a little after twelve, and she was supposed to be home by one, anyway.

Contrary to popular belief, Nate wasn't completely dead to the world. He'd noticed Blair lying all over that skinny, spiky-haired boy he'd never seen before, and he'd also noticed that Jenny looked kind of uncomfortable. But when things got weird, Nate tended to zone out and wait for somebody else to make a move.

"Okay," he said, snapping out of it. "Let's get out of here." The pot he'd brought with him was extremely mellow, and he didn't feel like going to a noisy club, anyway. After he dropped Jenny off he could always call Jeremy's cell and meet up with the boys at that bar on Rivington with the cozy back room where you could sit on the sofa and smoke pot and no one would bother you. "Hey," he called, rapping on the glass between the backseat and the driver. "Can you let us out?"

Blair smiled. Could it be that she had rubbed Nate so completely the wrong way that he had to get out because he couldn't face seeing her with her hands on another guy?

"Aw, Natie. Don't you guys want to come out with us?" Serena asked.

Nate shrugged. "I have to take her home," he said.

Jenny frowned. She didn't particularly like being referred to as "her." The limo driver stopped the car and opened the back door for them. Jenny hopped out and Nate clambered out after her. "'Bye!" she called brightly to everyone left inside.

Across the backseat Chuck smirked at her, his eyes slitted. "Too bad," he grunted.

Jenny wasn't sure what he meant, but she was pretty sure it was something perverted.

"See you!" Serena called back, the only other person who actually acknowledged their leaving. "Good luck on midterms!"

Nate and Jenny sat in silence during the taxi ride uptown. Nate was happy to watch the stores and restaurants whiz by, silently counting from one to twenty over and over in his stoned head. Jenny sat with her legs crossed around each other twice, fretting about what had gone wrong. It was mostly her fault, she reasoned. She was the one who'd wanted to take a ride in the limo in the first place.

The cab stopped in front of Jenny's building on Ninety-ninth and West End Avenue. She reached for the door handle.

"Hey," Nate said, touching her coat sleeve.

He couldn't let her go without saying good night. Whether he was baked into oblivion or not, he had good breeding, and with breeding came manners.

He kissed her on the cheek, his sandy hair brushing her skin. "Good night," he said with a sweet boyish smile.

Jenny smiled back, wanting desperately to forget the last hour and pretend that the night was ending as perfectly as it had begun.

"Good night," she said, suddenly reluctant to leave.

"Sleep tight," Nate added, his green eyes sparkling in the lamplight.

Aw.

He could be so incredibly adorable sometimes! Her heart brimming with true love, Jenny slammed the cab door closed and ran into the lobby of her building. Instead of taking the elevator, she ran all the way up the eight flights of stairs and burst into the apartment.

"Hey," her older brother, Dan, called to her. He was walking down the hall, carrying two mugs of Folgers instant coffee back to his bedroom.

"Hey."

Jenny peeled off her black faux fur coat and threw it at a chair in the corner. The coat hung on the back of the chair for a second and then slid to the floor. It wasn't like anyone would notice. The sprawling old four-bedroom apartment hadn't been cleaned properly in years.

"How was it?" Dan asked.

The star-shaped turquoise pendant Nate had given her hung at her throat. Jenny touched it for reassurance. "It was okay." She looked at the mugs in Dan's hands. "Is Vanessa still here?"

Dan nodded. He could sense that something was up. "Yeah. Want to come and hang out with us for a while?"

Jenny and Dan got along well, but he wasn't always this nice to her. "Okay," she agreed, following him down the hall to his room.

Vanessa was sitting on the bed, still in her black tank top

and tights. "Hey, Jennifer," she said, taking a mug of coffee from Dan. "You still want me to call you that, right?"

Jenny nodded. Only Nate and Vanessa called her Jennifer. Nate did it because that was how she'd introduced herself to him when they'd met in the park. And Vanessa did it because Jenny had asked her to.

Vanessa had always been nice to her. She'd always treated her with respect.

Dan's bed was all messed up, and the rest of Vanessa's clothes were on the floor. It was pretty clear to Jenny that Dan and Vanessa had been having sex. She stood in the doorway, embarrassed to go any further.

"Can I ask you a question?" she said finally. She didn't make it clear which one of them she was asking, because she didn't really mind if she got two answers.

"Go ahead," Vanessa said, sipping her coffee with her hands wrapped around the steaming mug.

"Can you tell me honestly what you think of Nate?"

Dan frowned. He and Nate didn't go to the same school, but by pure accident he'd wound up on a road trip up to Brown with Nate and Serena van der Woodsen and Nate's stoner friends last month. As far as he could tell, Nate was just a rich, good-looking pothead. There was nothing wrong with him, but he wasn't particularly special, either. It sort of killed Dan that his smart, beautiful sister was wasting her time with a guy who was bound to break her heart. But at the same time, Dan could see why Jenny was so enamored of Nate. He was older, for one thing, and he was the type of cute, popular boy every girl would want to go out with. At least, until she realized how boring he was.

At the back of Dan's mind was a nagging worry that Nate was pressuring Jenny to do things she wasn't ready to do, but

Jenny had come home almost an hour early and didn't look upset or anything, so he decided not to bring it up.

Vanessa shrugged. Nate was the type of preppy idiot she had no time for at all, but she didn't want to hurt Jenny's feelings by saying so. "I really don't know him, but all the girls at Constance are always talking about him. I guess he probably makes a good boyfriend."

Dan nodded. "Yeah." That was a decent way of putting it.

Jenny frowned. "Okay," she said, feeling more confused than ever. "I think I'm going to go take a shower."

She closed Dan's door and walked down the hall to her room. *He makes a good boyfriend*, she repeated to herself. What the hell was *that* supposed to mean? She didn't want just a good boyfriend. She wanted that thing Gustav Klimt had captured so perfectly in *The Kiss*. That radiant, electric, hold-me-tight-so-I-don't-fall-from-up-here-in-the-sky feeling of being *in love*.

Well, don't we all, sweetie?

you gotta be cruel to be kind

By the time the limo pulled up at Gorgon, the hot new club on the Lower East Side, Kati, Isabel, and Chuck had all fallen asleep in a sort of twisted heap of hair and scarves and purses and legs and coats on the black leather seat of the limo. Blair, Serena, Flow, Miles, and Aaron stood on the sidewalk looking down at them.

"Thank *God*," Blair said. If she had to listen to Kati or Isabel make one more mindless, stoned comment about the way everyone looked all purple or whatever, she was going to scream.

"They look like puppies," Serena observed.

"Want me to wake them up?" Miles offered.

"No!" the two girls squealed in unison.

"Hey Miles," Aaron said. "Isn't this one of your dad's clubs?"

Miles blushed and looked down at his shiny black Prada evening shoes. "Yeah." Blair thought it was actually kind of cute how embarrassed he was.

"Cool." Flow wound his bare fingers through Serena's gloved ones. "Ready to rock?"

Serena had that crazy, giddy feeling she got when she wasn't sure what was going to happen next. It was her favorite feeling. She squeezed his hand back. "Definitely."

They started walking toward the door of the club. The bouncer was already pulling aside the red velvet rope to let them in.

"Wait," Blair said, stopping as she remembered the gross comment Chuck had made earlier that evening. Now was her chance for some sweet, cheap revenge. "Who's got a pen?"

Flow pulled the black felt-tipped Sharpie he kept handy for signing autographs out from the inside breast pocket of his tuxedo jacket. Blair leaned into the limo, careful not to brush Chuck's nose with her coat sleeve as she wrote, *Take this loser HOME*, on his forehead. Then she slammed the limo door closed.

"Thanks," she said, handing the pen back to Flow. They started to walk past the enormous bearded bouncer and beyond the velvet rope.

"Um," Aaron said, hesitating. He flicked his Zippo open and closed. "I think I'm actually going to head home. I've got a lot of studying to do tomorrow."

Blair rolled her eyes. "So? So do I."

"Want to head back with me?" Aaron offered.

Blair glanced at Serena, who was adamantly shaking her head. "Nah," she answered.

"You sure you want to take off?" Miles asked Aaron. "It's pretty cool inside. And I can get us a private room."

"Awesome," Flow said appreciatively.

Aaron shook his head. He was the odd man out, and he knew it. "Yeah. I'll see you guys."

The four of them watched him walk down the street with his hands shoved in his tuxedo pants pockets, shirttails flapping out behind him. Then Flow grabbed Serena around the waist and picked her up, running with her toward the club door.

"Last one inside is a rotten egg!" she squealed.

Blair was about to take off after them when Miles grabbed her hand. "Hey. Do you mind if I do something before we go inside?"

Blair stared up at him. No, she didn't mind. After all, she was the one who'd put her hand on his leg inside the car.

Miles bent down and kissed her oh-so-gently on the mouth. It was a very polite, gentlemanly kiss. "I've been wanting to do that all night," he confessed with a shy smile.

Blair was trying to maintain Serena's devil-may-care attitude. She could do this. She could have random fun with a random boy who wasn't anything like Nate. Besides, after tonight she'd never have to see Miles again if she didn't want to.

She smiled coyly. "I guess we're the rotten eggs," she said, as she lifted her chin to kiss Miles again. And this time the kiss was anything but polite.

In three thousand words or less, write about a person who has inspired you in a profound way. Please demonstrate the effect of his or her life on yours as specifically as possible.

Blair Waldorf   Yale University Application Essay   December 18

Audrey Hepburn was born in Brussels on May 4, 1929, the daughter of a Dutch baroness and an Anglo-Irish businessman. The name on her birth certificate was Audrey Kathleen van Heemstra Ruston. When she was only three weeks old, she got sick with whooping cough and her heart stopped, but her determined mother revived her by spanking her. And even though she was only a baby, Audrey must have learned a lesson that day because for the rest of her life, even when she was sick, she lived her life to the fullest. Whenever I feel overwhelmed by the pressures of my AP exams or my crazy schedule, I think of Audrey and feel inspired.

I believe that if you apply yourself and work hard toward a goal, you will be rewarded. Audrey was rewarded by being discovered by . . .

gossipgirl.net

topics ◀ **previous** **next** ▶ **post a question** **reply**

hey people!

Are celebrities really more interesting than regular people?

We talk about them like we know them. We read everything we can get our hands on about them. We're sad for them when they're going through a tough breakup and happy for them when they get married or win an Oscar. We criticize their hairstyles, we notice when they gain or lose weight. We even fantasize about being friends with them. And sure, they have amazing clothes, lots of houses, and an open invitation to all the hot new restaurants. *But so do we.* The truth is, the only thing that makes famous people interesting is that they're famous. Unless of course they really *are* interesting, like . . . well, *me*, for instance.

Sightings

S and **Flow**—yes, *that* **Flow**, last seen receiving his MTV Music Award for best debut album—dancing like wild monkeys at **Gorgon** on Saturday night. Afterward, they were seen entering the **Tribeca Star**—to get a room, perchance? Naughty, naughty—I'm sure we'll read all about it in the tabloids tomorrow. **B** and a new boy we'll call **M**, also at **Gorgon**, sharing a romantic cigarette in the corner. **K**, **I**, and **C** looking disoriented as they stumbled out of a parked limo just before dawn, when the driver stopped for gas somewhere near the Third Avenue Bridge. Hopefully the driver was kind enough to take them home, where they belonged. **A** walking up Fifth Avenue wearing his tuxedo, looking sadder than a cute boy with dreadlocks deserves to look.

Your e-mail

Hey gg,
i know for a fact **flow** is gay. the only reason he's hanging with **S** is so people will think he's straight.
—snoopy

Dear snoopy,
I noticed at the Black-and-White that his tuxedo pants looked a little tight in the ass, so maybe you're right!
—GG

Yo GG,
I'm in **M**'s class at Bronxdale, and I've been crushing on him and his car for, like, two years. It's so cute how he's always drumming on his desk during class, and he drives this sweet old orange Porsche. I don't know what he's doing with **B**. She is a serious ho with an *h* and an *o*.
—Olive

Dear Olive,
See what happens when you stand idly by? The ho's get your guy. Ha! I'm a poet and I didn't even know it. Seriously, though, even if you never hook up with **M**, you could ask him to take you for a drive in that sweet old Porsche of his.
—GG

A last word about midterms

Don't cram. I know these are the last grades that count for college, but you *know* this stuff. And if you don't, it's too late to learn it. Just take a hot Dead Sea salt bath, put on your favorite pair of purple silk Versace pajamas, drink a glass of Cristal, paint your nails with that new color you picked up at the Chanel counter at Bendel's, and get your beauty sleep. You'll do a lot better that way than if you stay up late filling out index cards with stupid notes you won't even be able to read in the morning.

Good luck. I'll keep my fingers crossed for you!

You know you love me,

gossip girl

even celebrity girlfriends take midterms

It was Monday, the first day of midterm week, and the girls in the Constance Billard senior AP French class were sitting at their desks in a third-floor classroom, wearing their super-short gray wool uniform skirts, black TSE cashmere turtle-neck sweaters, black Wolford tights, and black suede Gucci loafers, hunched over their blank blue exam booklets, madly scribbling away. Blair sat in the front row, near the proctor, who happened to be her lame film teacher, Mr. Beckham, who she happened to despise because he'd given her a C on her last film paper. The paper had been on Woody Allen movies and how they don't speak to the greater American audience because they are only about New York and the neurotic people who live there. As it turned out, even though Mr. Beckham was from the Midwest, he was a Woody Allen fanatic. He'd called Blair's paper "condescending." What a prick.

The beginning of the exam was a series of questions that had to be answered in one concise, descriptive paragraph. The first question was *Qu'est-ce que vous voulez faire pendant votre temps libres?* "What do you like to do in your free time?"

That was beyond easy. Blair liked to shop for exquisitely

designed, expensive shoes, eat steak frites, drink Ketel One and tonic with Serena, and smoke a lot. In the summers she liked to play tennis. She used to like kissing Nate on her bed while *Breakfast at Tiffany's* was on the DVD player in the background, but now she didn't do that anymore. She was too busy doing all those other things.

The next question was *Decrivez votre famille.* "Describe your family."

Blair let out an exasperated sigh. She was practically fluent in French, so she knew the words for "vain homosexual," "stupid flake," and "overweight, tacky loser," which was how she would truthfully describe her father, her mother, and her stepfather. But Madame Rogers, her French teacher, had a major pole up her ass and no sense of humor at all, so it was unlikely she'd be impressed by Blair's description. Instead, Blair generously described her father as "a handsome fellow whose favorite hobby is the same as mine: buying shoes"; her mother as "a good-natured blond woman who would forget her own name unless someone reminded her"; and her stepfather as "a jolly man with a loud laugh and unusual taste in clothes." Her little brother, Tyler, was easy: "He might grow up to be cute, but his best friends are his PlayStation 2 and his eighties record collection." That left Aaron. Blair paused for a moment. She liked Aaron, even though he'd been acting kind of quiet and sullen lately. On the stepbrother scale, he could have been so much worse. She smiled to herself and wrote, *My new stepbrother, Aaron, will probably save the world.* There. That was just about the nicest thing she'd ever said about anyone.

The next question was *Imaginez qu'un djinn apparaît sur votre épaule pour vous dire qu'il vous accordera un seul souhait. Quel serait votre souhait??*

Blair tapped her number two pencil against the wooden

desk. What would she wish for? She wished she would get into Yale, obviously. And she wished her mother and Cyrus would stay on their honeymoon forever so she wouldn't have to live with them or see them kissing and fondling each other in public all the time. She wished Nate would move to Antarctica so she wouldn't ever have to bump into him or his little girlfriend again. She also really wanted a pair of tan leather boots with skinny four-inch heels; she just hadn't found the right pair yet. And a sheepskin jacket. And a fox fur hat with earflaps.

Blair didn't really mind that her father was gay, but she wished he'd find a boyfriend to live with in New York instead of France so he could take her shopping more often. And she wished Serena was in AP French so they could sit next to each other during their exam and pass notes about all the crazy stories in the papers today about Serena and Flow. She also kind of wished she and Nate had gone ahead and had sex when they were together so she wouldn't still be a virgin. And she kind of wished she hadn't stayed up so late on Saturday night with Miles and Flow and Serena, because she was still a little hungover from it. Plus Miles had called her twice yesterday and left messages on her machine, even though she had specifically given him a fake number so she would never have to hear from him again. Not that she was even considering calling him back.

Saturday night had been fun, but the last fucking thing she needed right now was a new boyfriend.

Mr. Beckham cleared his throat noisily, and Blair lifted her eyes from her exam paper and stared him. He had yellow hair. Not blond yellow, but yellow like a person's snot when they're seriously sick. Their eyes met, and then Mr. Beckham did a weird thing: He blushed.

Excusez-moi?

Blair turned away, horrified. Her foot jiggled nervously as she looked at the question. *Vous avez une desire. Que desirez vous?*

She wished very much that her skeevy film studies teacher who she thought hated her hadn't just looked like he might actually have a crush on her. She wished she were on the beach right now instead of freezing her ass off in an under-heated classroom. She wished she'd eaten breakfast, because she was starving. She wished a lot of things, but one answer would have to do.

She wrote down the thing about getting into Yale, even though it seemed totally redundant for a senior in high school to write about wanting to get into college, but she'd rather be boring than reveal any juicy personal details to Madame Rogers, anyway. Then she drew a little high-heeled boot in the margin of her blue exam book and looked up at Mr. Beckham again. He was still staring at her, his cheeks a gross shade of purpley-red. *What* was he doing? Plotting her murder, or imagining what she would look like in her underwear? Blair looked away, disgusted. She glanced at her platinum Cartier tank watch. Another fucking hour to go. Next question.

Two floors below Blair, in the Constance Billard School auditorium, Serena was toiling over her American history exam.

Not. Serena wasn't exactly the toiling type.

She had already counted the number of split ends in the end of her ponytail—nine—and she'd answered the question about the English involvement in World War II with a *very* short essay about how during wartime there were shortages of everything and English women had to give up wearing stockings because there was no nylon available. Instead, those fearless, industrious, fashion-conscious women had painted lines down the backs of their legs to make it look like they were wearing them.

Serena sighed. In those days a girl could probably spend a night out with a guy and not have her picture plastered all over the gossip pages the next day. Pictures of Serena and Flow at Gorgon had appeared in the *Post*, *Entertainment Weekly*, *People*, *Women's Wear Daily*, and countless Web sites, all naming them "the new 'it' couple."

It was so ridiculous. She'd kissed Flow good-bye in the wee hours outside the Tribeca Star Hotel bar on Sunday morning, and he'd gone off to catch a private plane down to Baja, where he was reshooting some scenes for the video for 45's new song, "Life of Krime," before he went away for Christmas. He'd been incredibly sweet and they'd had an awesome time that night, but they very definitely were not a couple. A couple meant you saw each other every day. It meant you were in love. And though she and Flow might have been a little in *lust*, they were very definitely not in love, despite the fact that he had already sent her flowers.

Three dozen very-hard-to-find black tulips, to be exact.

Serena was used to getting gifts from guys, so the flowers didn't faze her, as long as Flow didn't start sending her things every day. Sometimes a guy could go a little overboard. Take Dan Humphrey for example. He'd followed Serena around like a puppy dog when she'd returned from boarding school in the fall, and he'd even written her poems that were so lovesick and serious, they were kind of scary. Serena really liked Dan, but he was a little too intense. Lucky for her, he'd hooked up with Vanessa, who was equally intense, and they made a great couple. But Serena wasn't interested in being matched up with anyone. She treasured her independence, her ability to follow her whimsy and do what she pleased. She was a spur-of-the-moment kind of girl—couplehood would only cramp her style.

Serena stared at the next question. *When did the American armed forces enter World War II, and why?*

A more pertinent question was *When was she ever going to use this knowledge??* The answer was pretty obvious: *never!* Who cared about what had happened in the past when the future lay ahead of her with fabulous surprises and untold craziness hiding behind every curve and bend?

Someone tapped her on the shoulder and Serena looked up. It was Mr. Hanson, her Latin teacher and the proctor for the history exam. He was tall and thin and had a mustache that was always so exactly the same length, the girls at Constance were all convinced it must be a falsie.

"What?" Serena said, startled. She knew she'd been spacing out, but she couldn't get in trouble for that during a written exam, could she? "Did I do something wrong?"

Then she noticed that Mr. Hanson was smiling under his mustache.

He shoved a copy of the *Post* into her hands. It was turned to Page Six, the celebrity gossip page, where there was a huge picture of Serena and Flow getting into a cab after leaving Gorgon on Saturday night. "I'm so sorry to interrupt, but I noticed you were finished with your exam, and I was just wondering if it would be possible for you to ask Flow to sign this," he whispered. "I'm such a huge fan. And it would be great if you would sign it, too."

Serena blinked. First of all, she'd had no idea Mr. Hanson was cool enough to even know who Flow *was*. Second of all, she had no intention of asking Flow for anything. And third of all—*Hel-lo?* She was nowhere near finished with her exam!

"Flow's in Baja," she whispered back. "Is it okay if I just sign it?" She glanced around the room self-consciously. Most of the other girls had stopped writing and were either staring at her and Mr. Hanson or chatting amongst themselves.

"I heard Flow and Serena are engaged," Nicki Button told her friend Alicia Edwards. "They're getting married on New Year's Eve, in Vegas. At the Bellagio."

"The *Post* said they met at the Black-and-White on Saturday," Isabel Coates told Kati Farkas. "But that's so not true."

"They met in rehab last year, right?" said Kati. "Flow's been in rehab, like, twelve times. But so has she."

Serena signed her name and handed the paper back to Mr. Hanson, hoping he wouldn't give her a bad grade in Latin now that she hadn't gotten him Flow's autograph.

"Thanks," he whispered, examining her signature. He smiled excitedly. "I'm sure this is going to be worth a fortune one day!"

"No problem," Serena said, humoring him. The buzz in the room was getting louder and louder.

"All right, girls. Back to work," Mr. Hanson called sternly as he went back to his desk at the front of the room.

Serena looked down at her exam paper again. *When did the American armed forces enter World War II, and why?*

But before she could even begin to answer the question, she was swarmed by a dozen of her classmates, all clutching copies of the *Post* for her to sign. Mr. Hanson couldn't very well tell them to stop when he was the one who'd started it in the first place.

"All right," he said, ignoring Serena's pleading look. "I'll give everyone five extra minutes on your exam. Five minutes, and then I want you back in your seats."

"Me first!" cried Rain Hoffstetter, shoving her copy of the *Post* at Serena.

"No, me!" Laura Salmon shouted, pushing Rain out of the way.

Serena giggled to herself in amazement. When she'd returned from boarding school two months ago, she'd been considered a leper. And now everyone wanted her autograph?

She hesitated, pen poised above the photograph in Laura's copy of the paper. Then she wrote in her trademark loopy scrawl, *You know you love me, Serena.*

sex, love, and frankenstein

The senior English exam at Riverside Prep was notoriously long and difficult, but Dan wasn't worried. He had read Mary Shelley's *Frankenstein* twice and had most of the Keats poems in his anthology memorized. Besides, he could write an A-worthy English essay in his sleep.

After deconstructing "Ode to a Nightingale" as thoroughly as he could, he flipped to the back of his blue exam booklet and started writing a new poem that hopefully would turn into something he could send along with his college applications. Dan generally never wrote anything but angst-ridden love poems. This one was called "For Vanessa."

> *Paper cuts*
> *slicing lemons*
> *saltwater in my eyes*

He was experimenting with a new form of free verse, and he wasn't quite sure whether it made any sense.

> *Your face*
> *a nut*

you soothe my cuts
and oil my engine

Oil my engine? No, that sounded too sexual, and he didn't want to give Vanessa any ideas in case he actually showed her the poem. What he meant was, she inspired him. Dan stared at the words and tried to think of a better way to put it. Then he tore the piece of paper out of the book and crumpled it up into a ball. Why couldn't he ever write anything good anymore?

Dan felt somebody watching him and glanced to his left where Chuck Bass, one of the biggest dicks in his class, was sitting. In seventh grade, Chuck had been one of the shortest boys in the class. He wore horn-rimmed glasses and brown corduroy suits and looked like he had to go to the bathroom all the time. He and Dan had seventh grade English together, and the teacher had asked them to write a poem in class about a body part. Chuck was terrible at creative writing, and he'd passed Dan a note begging Dan to write a poem for him. Writing came easy to Dan, so he'd written the first thing that came to mind, a poem about his hands and all they did for him in the course of a day. He'd given the poem to Chuck to turn in, and then dashed off another poem about his mouth that wasn't half as good. Chuck had gotten an A+ on the hands poem and a note from the teacher that said, *See what you can do when you put your mind to it?* ☺, while Dan had gotten a B on his mouth poem and a note from the teacher that said, *I know you can do better.* ☹

At first, Dan didn't mind. At least he'd helped out a kid who seemed like he really needed it. But within a year Chuck grew a foot and a half taller, started shaving and wearing his signature monogrammed pinky ring and navy blue cashmere scarf, and turned into a serious asshole, especially when it came to girls. He'd even tried to molest Dan's little sister, Jenny, in a bathroom stall at a party last month. Dan had made it very clear that he hated Chuck's guts, but Chuck didn't seem to care. Every now and then he would still ask Dan for help in English, and Dan would have to tell him to fuck off, *again*.

Right now Chuck was staring at Dan's blue book, trying to read his essay on "Ode to a Nightingale." Dan turned to a fresh page and wrote, *CAN YOU READ THIS, ASSHOLE? GO FUCK YOURSELF!* in giant black capital letters. Chuck squinted at Dan's blue book and then looked up and gave Dan the finger.

NO, fuck YOU! Dan wrote, and underlined it twice.

Before going on to the next question, Dan reread some lines from "Ode to a Nightingale" on his exam sheet.

Darkling I listen; and for many a time
I have been half in love with easeful Death

There was a perfect beginning to a poem for Vanessa. She was his darkling. And it was true, Dan *was* half in love with death, the way he chain-smoked, and rarely ate, and drank way, way too much coffee. Vanessa kept him sane. She kept him alive.

Dan picked up his pen again and tried to think of a more succinct, poetic way to write the same thing Keats had written, only different. But no matter how hard he tried, he couldn't think of another way of saying the same thing that was even half as good. Instead he read the next question on the exam.

In class we have discussed the various symbolic meanings of Mary Shelley's man-made, manlike creation, Frankenstein. But what does Frankenstein mean to you?

Dan stared at the glowing red Exit sign over the gym door, thinking. He'd always thought Frankenstein was scary, but also very beautiful in a way. Frankenstein didn't mean to harm anyone, but he couldn't help it—he was a monster. In a way, he was like love itself: horrible and wonderful, terrifying and liberating, thrilling and sad, all at the same time.

Trembling with creative energy, Dan flipped to a fresh page in the back of his blue book and wrote *For Vanessa* again at the top of the page. Then he wrote the first line: *You are my Frankenstein.*

Oh, dear. Do we even *want* to know what the second line was?

Vanessa sat at the back of the Constance Billard School auditorium taking the same history exam Serena was taking. She'd finished the exam forty-five minutes early, and now, while her mindless classmates were all swarming around Serena like little worker bees around their queen because Serena happened to have been photographed with that vapid, tone-deaf poster boy of a lead singer over the weekend, Vanessa was mapping out a route for a film tour of the city that she hoped to hand in to NYU as part of her application. Screw Page Six. She was going to document the *real* things that went on in the city, the truly interesting stuff that happened right under people's noses while they were busy reading Page Six.

First, she wanted to get up before dawn and film the fishermen down in the harbor delivering their fish to the Fulton Fish Market. The smell of fish made her gag, but it was one of those perfect things: She could trace one fish's journey from the boat to the market, where it would be sold for, like, thirty-two cents a pound, to some restaurant uptown, where it would be served encrusted in pistachio nuts with a side of red potatoes and wild mushroom butter for twenty-nine dollars a plate. Some anorexic twice-divorced Park Avenue woman would order it, eat only a few tiny bites, and then the rest of it would get thrown away.

That was exactly the kind of irony Vanessa lived for: the

bittersweet kind. She was a pessimist and Dan was a romantic, which was why, no matter how much she loved him, she couldn't see why Dan had gotten so worked up about them having sex. The way she saw it, the longer Dan waited and the more he blew sex out of proportion, writing poems about it and worrying himself sleepless, the more he was destined for disappointment. But she couldn't think of a gentle way to make him see that, other than to just tie him down and rip his clothes off. Which might not be such a bad idea.

Vanessa smiled to herself and turned her thoughts back to her film essay.

After the fish market she wanted to spend the day with one of those bicycle cops who were always riding their bikes in pairs around Central Park, and who never seemed to care that all the kids in Sheep Meadow were getting high and drinking beer underage. What she wanted to find out was, did they ever arrest anyone, or were they just trying to build muscle tone in their legs with all that riding? Actually, the police department probably wouldn't let her film the bike cops without some kind of permit, but it was a nice idea anyway.

Finally, she wanted to hang out with a hot-dog vendor. See his house, his family, his dog. See if he had any regular customers. See if maybe while he waited for people to come buy hot dogs he read some very challenging book, like *Gravity's Rainbow*, by Thomas Pynchon, and dreamed of being a leader of men someday. Or maybe he was just happy being a hot-dog vendor and eating free hot dogs all day.

A movement at the front of the room caught Vanessa's eye. The Constance lemmings were dispersing from around Serena's chair.

"Thank you, girls. And thank you, Serena," Mr. Hanson called. "Ten more minutes."

Vanessa watched as Serena went back to fervently splitting her split ends.

Serena and Dan were both supposed to have starred in Vanessa's *War and Peace* film that October. But then Dan had acted like such an idiot around Serena that Vanessa couldn't stand it, so she'd asked a girl who could barely act to play the female lead instead. Serena had been into Dan, too, but only for about five seconds. And before Serena could do too much damage, Vanessa had stormed in with her shaved head and black turtleneck and combat boots to mend his broken heart.

Vanessa uncrossed her legs and then crossed them again. The thought of rescuing Dan from a broken heart made her want to have sex with him even more. She sighed impatiently. Over break she and Dan were going to spend a lot of time together with very little adult supervision. Whether he was ready or not, it was only a matter of time before they did it.

See? Despite Vanessa's tough look and disdain for almost everyone else in the human race, she was just another curious seventeen-year-old girl. We're all the same.

n can't get b's ass out of his head

Nate was eating lunch at Jackson Hole with Anthony Avuldsen, Charlie Dern, and Jeremy Scott Tompkinson in the hour between his calculus and chemistry exams. The calc exam had been a total bitch, and they were all loading up on burgers and fries and Cokes to make it through chem, which was probably going to be even worse. Nate was thinking about how the restaurant should invest in some ceiling fans to get rid of the deep-fried-onion–fart odor lingering in the air. He was also thinking about Jenny and Blair in the sort of nonspecific, unworried way he tended to think about most things.

He hadn't heard from Jennifer since Saturday night, which was kind of strange, since she usually sent him cryptic little text messages on his cell phone or sweet little e-mails to his St. Jude's School e-mail address. Maybe she was just busy studying for midterms.

Nate pushed his plate away and pulled his Nokia phone out of his pocket. It wouldn't hurt for him to send her a text message, just to keep her spirits up during exams.

Aw, how thoughtful.

Gd lk! he wrote. *Thurs pm il tke u xmas shppg x N.*

Jeremy stretched his skinny arms overhead and rolled his

head around to unkink his neck. "Hey, who're you texting, man?" He was a small, gawky kid who was so thin he had trouble keeping his pants up, but he made up for it with his trendy English rock star haircut and stoner-boy way of talking.

Nate shrugged. "None of your business."

Anthony shoved a handful of cold, ketchup-soaked fries into his mouth. He played on just about every sports team at St. Jude's, so he could eat fries all day and still look buff. "Hey, I noticed Blair was looking pretty hot on Saturday night," he said.

Nate nodded as an image of Blair's tennis-taut ass in her tight black dress surfaced in his mind. She *had* looked good.

"Course she's not stacked like Jennifer," Anthony added.

The boys had stopping making fun of Nate for going out with a ninth grader a while ago, but every now and then they made a reference to Jenny's enormous chest. It was kind of hard not to.

Nate smiled. Then he frowned, trying to remember what Jennifer had looked like on Saturday, but all that came to mind was a mess of brown curls, her stupendous cleavage, and her shy smile.

He took a few gulps of Coke, squinting his gorgeous green eyes and thinking hard.

Which was a *very* rare occurrence indeed.

It was strange, but Nate had never sat down and actually compared the two girls. He really liked Jennifer a lot— she was less demanding than Blair and kind of left him to his own thoughts, while Blair always wanted to know what he was thinking or where he was going and who with. Jenny didn't put any pressure on him the way Blair had, like forcing him to apply to Yale so they could live together off campus or giving him expensive presents so he'd feel compelled to return the gesture and buy her something, too. And Jenny had those incredible breasts, while Blair's were just sort of *there*. Nice, but nothing spectacular.

Despite Blair's shortcomings, though, he'd always felt like they really *knew* each other—after all, they'd grown up together. And the whole time they'd been going out, he'd felt like they were moving toward something. There was a destination, like the red pin he stuck in his nautical charts when he sailed his boat into harbor somewhere. The destination was partly sex—they'd done everything but, so it was an obvious next step. But it was also partly something less specific. Their lives were moving forward at the same pace, separately, but together, like the pontoons on a Hobie Cat. They were both seventeen. They were both graduating this June. They were both going to college next year.

He and Jennifer were on totally separate courses, and unfortunately sex wasn't even on the horizon. She was only fourteen. Next year, and for two more years after that, she'd be putting on her uniform and going to Constance Billard every day while he was at college doing who knows what. Most guys would be put off by the age difference, but Nate found it sort of comforting. While he was drifting in the uncharted waters of the future, Jenny would be securely anchored at home. He could text her, or call her, or come back and see her, and nothing would have changed.

Charlie stabbed his uneaten pickle with his fork and flopped it onto Nate's plate like a dead fish. "You look like you're jonesing. Think you can make it through chem?"

Nate looked up and squeezed the little plastic bag of pot

in his pocket. He glanced at his watch. "How about a quick smoke before we go in?"

The other three boys nodded eagerly, and Nate smiled and stood up. He felt like he'd worked something out in his head, although he wasn't quite sure what. "Right on," he said. "Let's do it."

maybe guys are like clothes

While Constance Billard's juniors and seniors were starting their second midterm exam, Jenny was in health class, discussing love, sex, shampoo, and the physiognomies of boys, among other things.

Eleven freshman girls sat in a circle on the floor beneath a sunny window in a cozy nook of a room that had been specifically designed by the school for intimate classes like ninth-grade health. On the floor was a plush crimson carpet instead of the institutional puke green one that covered the floors of the rest of the school. The walls were painted a cheerful cornflower blue, bordered in crisp linen white. There was a small, freestanding chalkboard with plenty of colored chalk for the teacher to draw diagrams; and, most importantly, there were no desks, allowing the girls to relax their bodies and really talk about what was on their minds.

The class was taught by Ms. Doherty, the New Age hippie dance teacher, who was twenty-five, with a gorgeous, yoga-toned body, long auburn hair, and a pale face that was always completely free of makeup. She was the only teacher in the gym department who wasn't totally butch, and the girls would have loved her easygoing, open manner if it weren't for her tendency to talk about embarrassing body parts like they were the family dog. Ms. Doherty let the girls choose the topics for discussion, so they usually spent the bulk of class time talking about *boys*.

"I honestly don't understand how we're supposed to meet people of the opposite sex when we spent ninety percent of our time in an all-girls environment," Kim Swanson complained. She ran her hands carefully over her perfectly blow-dried blond hair, which she'd been getting highlighted every other month at the John Barrett Salon since fourth grade.

Jenny sat next to Kim, marveling at how perfect *everything* about her was. Her French manicured nails, her golden beige tanning salon tan, her subtly applied Chanel mascara, eye shadow, and lip gloss, the square Cartier diamond studs in her ears, and her crisp white Agnés B. oxford shirt. Maybe if Kim didn't spend so much time grooming herself, she'd have more free time to meet boys.

Ms. Doherty smiled her placid, benevolent smile. "I know it's hard, Kim," she said sympathetically. "All I can suggest is, get involved in some of those coed interschool activities like drama and glee club. And if your friends have friends who are boys, don't be shy—ask them to introduce you!"

"Ms. Doherty, do you think you have to be in love with a guy to be with him?" Jessica Soames asked. Jessica looked exactly like Snow White from the fairy tale, with thick black hair, red, full lips and long-lashed gray eyes, although she was definitely *not* pure as the driven snow. Jessica had gotten her period in fourth grade and the rumor was she'd lost her virginity in sixth. Originally, *she* had had the biggest chest in the class, but over the past year Jenny's chest had far exceeded Jessica's.

Ms. Doherty tucked a stray auburn hair behind her ear and smoothed out her wispy auburn eyebrows, obviously trying to think of a tactful way of answering the question while drawing out further discussion. But before she could say anything, little Jenny Humphrey piped up.

"Yes, definitely. I mean, maybe it takes a while for both of you to realize you're in love, but if you aren't, then I think you should break up."

The entire class, including Ms. Doherty, stared at her. Ms. Doherty was staring because Jenny Humphrey never spoke in class and she'd had no idea Jenny was so opinionated. The girls were staring because they all knew Jenny had managed to snag Nate Archibald away from Blair Waldorf, which was really quite amazing, and there was no way she could have done it unless she was putting out, big time. Was Jenny Humphrey secretly even sluttier than Jessica Soames? And was she now admitting it?

When Jenny noticed everyone looking at her, she blushed. "I mean, I don't think you have to break up if you haven't said 'I love you' to each other yet, because maybe you still like hanging out together and everything and you're just waiting for the right time to say it."

Ms. Doherty nodded and smiled her lipstick-free smile. Love was one of her favorite topics. "The first time you fall in love, it can be hard to recognize. Some people even mistake it for the flu!"

A few of the girls giggled and Jenny smiled to herself. She knew what Ms. Doherty meant. Sometimes Jenny felt so dizzy and faint when she was with Nate, she could easily have been coming down with the pneumonia or something.

Ms. Doherty went on. "But I also don't think you have to be in love to have a relationship. You're only fourteen. It's not like you're going to marry the guy, right? You're just learning how to be with people. It's like trying on clothes. You have to try all different styles and sizes to see which ones suit you the best."

Jenny frowned. She didn't want to try on all different styles and sizes. She only wanted Nate.

"Wait, are we talking about *having sex* with someone you aren't in love with, or just, like, hanging out?" Alicia Armstrong asked craftily. She twisted her pink leather armband around and around on her wrist. "Cuz, like, I really think you should be in love if you're going to have sex."

"Oh, definitely," Jenny agreed quickly, blushing again.

The rest of the class stared at her again. So was she admitting to having sex with Nate Archibald or denying it?

Jenny hadn't even been talking about sex, but now she realized that was what Jessica meant when she'd said "be with" a guy. She pulled a strand of yarn out of the red carpet. For her, sex wasn't even the issue. It was love. How long should she wait before she told Nate that she loved him? Or should she wait for him to say it?

She raised her hand again, but Azaria Muniz raised hers first. "Ms. Doherty, is it true you should alternate between different shampoos when you wash your hair to avoid buildup?" Azaria had wavy honey-colored hair that hung down to her butt, and her locker was full of hair products.

Ms. Doherty looked at Azaria blankly. "Don't quote me on this, but I think as long as you use a good product with all-natural ingredients that don't cause buildup, you can use the same shampoo every time." She smiled and turned back to Jenny, eager to get back to the subject of love. "Yes, Jenny? You had your hand up?"

Jenny looked up at the ceiling, choosing her words carefully. But before she could even start, Jessica rudely interrupted her.

"Is it true that all the feeling is in the end part of the

penis?" Jessica asked, her black eyebrows knitted together seriously, as if she were asking a question about the discovery of the atom.

The rest of the class erupted into giggles. Jessica always asked the most outrageous questions, but they were all secretly glad when she did.

"Jessica, please don't interrupt your classmates," Ms. Doherty said evenly. "Briefly, the answer to your question is yes, the tip of the penis is very sensitive, but sensitivity varies from penis to penis." She turned back to Jenny. "Jenny, you were saying?"

Jenny let out a snort and her cheeks turned pink. *Penis, penis, penis!* The word always made her giggle.

"Yes?" Ms. Doherty prompted.

Jenny covered her mouth with her hand. "Oh, it was nothing."

Jessica's eyes narrowed. "What's so funny, Jenny? Is that Nate's most sensitive part? The tip?"

Jenny stopped smiling and crossed her arms over her chest. Her whole body blushed a dark, flaming red.

"Remember, Jessica—no naming names," Ms. Doherty cautioned. She readjusted her legs in the lotus position and cleared her throat. "I want to remind you girls again that our discussions are all confidential. Nothing said here will be repeated outside the group."

Yeah, *right.* Then how come everyone in the entire school knew that Alicia Armstrong didn't use tampons because her parents thought that if she did, she wouldn't be a virgin anymore?

Jenny wasn't stupid. She knew that whatever she said would definitely be repeated, so she decided it was safer not to say anything than to say something that might be taken the wrong way.

"I remember the first time I saw an actual penis," Jessica burst out, sending the rest of the class into a giggling frenzy once more. "I was so freaked out!"

Ms. Doherty smiled her Zenlike smile. Not even Jessica Soames was going to cause her to lose her temper. "Remember," she said. "This is a place to ask questions. . . ."

"I don't understand the whole erection thing. How exactly does that happen?" Kim Swanson asked.

"Is it true that guys always have them first thing when they wake up in the morning?" asked Roni Chang.

Ms. Doherty sighed. As she began to tactfully answer their questions, Jenny tuned them all out, preferring to stick to the subject of love.

If boys were like clothes, the way Ms. Doherty said, then Nate was like her first pair of Diesel jeans that she'd bought and only worn on special occasions because they were so nice she didn't want to get them dirty. But the more she wore them and the more she washed them, the better they fit, until it got so she couldn't live without them—they were the perfect fit. And if she knew so absolutely how she felt about him, then what was the harm in telling him?

an extraordinary answer
to an ordinary question

Blair had handed in a draft of her Yale admissions essay earlier that morning, and when the AP French and AP calculus exams were finally over, she dropped by Constance Billard's college advisor's office to see if Ms. Glos had read it yet.

Ms. Glos was sorting through her files, her surprisingly long, trim legs crossed neatly at the knees. "Oh, hello, Blair. Why don't you sit down?"

Blair narrowed her eyes and stared critically at Ms. Glos's ugly brown orthopedic shoes. What a waste to have such great legs for an older woman and absolutely no taste in shoes. She sat down in the hard wooden chair across from Ms. Glos's desk.

"I read your essay," said Ms. Glos. She thumbed through the stack of files on her desk until she found the one marked Waldorf. Then she pursed her thin lips and dabbed at her nose with a tissue. Ms. Glos was always getting nosebleeds and was thought to have some rare contagious disease. All the girls were afraid to touch the handouts she gave them.

Blair raised her dark, neatly plucked eyebrows. "And?"

Ms. Glos looked up. Her mouse brown hair curled under at the bottom, just grazing her chin. It looked exactly the same every time Blair saw her and was so obviously a wig. "I think you'd better take another stab at it if you're really serious about getting into Yale."

It took a moment for Blair to register what the college advisor had said. "But—"

Ms. Glos opened Blair's file and stabbed at the stapled pages inside with a long, nasty yellow fingernail. "This is a perfectly adequate essay on the life of Audrey Hepburn," she said. "But it doesn't say anything about *you*. You need to show Yale that you can write well, that you can think creatively, *and* that you can give an extraordinary answer to an ordinary question." She handed the essay back to Blair.

Blair held the six stapled pages between her thumb and forefinger, her temples throbbing. She was dying to tell Ms. Glos to fuck off and buy herself a new wig while she was at it, but she knew the college advisor was extremely good at her job, and if anyone could help her get into Yale, Ms. Glos could.

"Okay," she said, tersely. "I'll try again."

"Good girl. Try not to be so literal. *Show* them how much you admire Audrey Hepburn movies rather than *telling* them."

Blair nodded and stood up. She smoothed out her skirt, trying to maintain her composure in the face of such outrageous insult, behaving exactly as she imagined Audrey would behave. "Have a nice Christmas," she added politely.

Ms. Glos dabbed at her nose with a tissue again and smiled. "Merry Christmas, Blair."

Blair pulled the college advisor's office door shut behind her and dropped her disease-tainted essay into the metal wastebasket in the hallway with an irritated sigh. So much for fun on the beach in St. Barts. Serena would have to fend for herself, because Blair was going to have to spend the entire fucking vacation indoors, rewriting her Yale essay. She felt like writing, *Just let me the fuck in!* on a piece of paper and sending it off to the Yale admissions office, but considering the fact that she'd told her interviewer her whole life story and then kissed him, that probably wasn't such a great idea.

She started up the stairs to the fourth floor to retrieve her sky blue Marc Jacobs coat from her locker, bumping into Kati Farkas and Isabel Coates on their way downstairs.

"How was your French exam?" asked Kati. It had rained that morning as she was walking to school, and her strawberry blond hair was frizzing out all over the place.

Blair thought Kati looked like a poodle that had been struck by lightning. She shrugged. "Stupid." She shook her hair away from her face impatiently. She was so sick of talking about grades and school and AP exams, she thought she might puke.

Isabel combed her fingers through her short dark ponytail and lifted her chin. Blair always got so annoyingly superior when she talked about grades. "I know it sounds sort of geeky, but I actually went to Mr. Noble's history review session yesterday, and I think it really helped. I mean, I thought the exam was rather easy."

And you are rather *annoying,* Blair noted. Isabel's father was a TV actor who mostly did voice-overs and had a fake British accent. Isabel tended to imitate him, which was why she said things like "rather easy" instead of "totally stupid," making her sound, well, totally stupid.

Kati nodded. "It was short, too. But did you see Serena? She didn't even finish. She was still sitting there, like, staring at her hair when we left."

Of course she left out the part about Serena signing autographs. No way was she going to admit to Blair that she'd actually asked Serena for one.

"I'm sure she did fine," Blair said loyally. Serena never

studied and wasn't in any AP classes, but she always managed to scrape by well enough by participating in class and writing semidecent papers. She was smart—all the girls at Constance were—but her teachers had been complaining about her not working up to her potential since she was in second grade. Deep down, Blair relished the fact that Serena was so unacademic. It would be totally impossible to be friends with her if she were that gorgeous *and* got straight A's.

"So what happened with you and that guy Miles?" Isabel asked.

She couldn't believe these two. The last time she'd seen Kati and Isabel, they'd been passed out drunk in the back of a limo and Blair had totally ditched them. Now they were acting like they wanted to be her best friends again. But Blair didn't feel like chitchatting with them about some guy she was probably never going to see again so they could spread gossip about her all over the school.

"Nothing, really," she replied nonchalantly.

"Oooh," Isabel cooed. "She's being all *secretive*. That means *something* must have happened."

Blair rolled her eyes. "Whatever."

"So what did Ms. Glos say about your Yale essay?" Kati asked nosily.

That was the thing about going to a small girls' school: Everyone knew everything about everyone. It drove Blair *insane*.

"She liked it," Blair lied. She started up the stairs again, her little ruby ring tapping the metal banister noisily as she walked. "See you guys later. I have to start studying for English."

"Wait!" Isabel called.

Blair turned around and waited. "What?"

"Is it true Serena and Flow are engaged?"

Blair could barely contain her laughter. She knew she should tell them the truth, but it would be so much more interesting not to.

"Yeah," she said, shaking her head with a disbelieving smile. "Isn't it crazy?"

The two girls glanced at each other, clearly thrilled that they'd gotten confirmation on this groundbreaking gossip from a very reliable source.

"So is she still going to St. Barts with you?" Kati demanded.

Blair nodded and spun her ruby ring around on her little finger. "We're going to plan the wedding while we're there."

"Oh, that sounds like such fun!" Isabel declared in her most obnoxious English accent. She glanced at Kati and then back at Blair. "Do you think she'll ask us to be bridesmaids?"

Blair turned and glided effortlessly up the stairs like Audrey in her gorgeous Givenchy gown during the fashion show scene in *Funny Face*. "Maybe," she called. "If you're really, really nice to her."

Just because she had to spend her entire break rewriting her Yale essay didn't mean she couldn't have a little fun at the same time.

hey people!

Okay, so we made it through midterms—now it's time to splurge.

A Christmas wish list

1 Fendi fox fur hat, even though it will probably get left behind in a taxi one late night

1 Coach fringed suede wristlet bag, good for going out with only keys, credit card, and lip gloss. What else would anyone need?

A year's worth of appointments at the Elizabeth Arden Red Door Salon for facials, eyebrow and bikini waxes, seaweed wraps, haircuts, and highlights.

1 pair tan leather boots. 1 pair dark brown suede boots. 1 pair knee-high black boots. All from Stephane Kelian and all with four-inch heels. There's no such thing as too many pairs of boots.

1 Fendi sheepskin coat.

1 extra-large box of Godiva dark chocolate truffles—my weakness. Well, one of them, anyway.

1 TSE white cashmere bathrobe and matching cashmere slipper-socks

All the classic Hitchcock movies on DVD

Acceptance to all colleges applied to

A life-changing New Year's Eve!!

Sightings

B taking out every book on **Audrey Hepburn** in the mid-Manhattan library. **A** and his friend **M** walking A's boxer (that's a dog, not a prize-fighter) past the **Constance Billard School for Girls** and looking up into the octagonal first-floor windows—for whom, I wonder? **S** offering her doorman a fishbowl full of baby barracudas. Are *Flow*'s daily deliveries getting a bit much? **N** getting high with his friends in **Sheep Meadow**. **J** making a fabulous, glittery Christmas card for **N** in art class. **D** chucking one of his precious little black books in a trash can on Broadway. Isn't writer's block a bitch? **V** stalking some poor innocent hot-dog vendor in **Washington Square Park**. **K** and **I** fighting over a fox fur hat in **Intermix**.

Your e-mail

Dear "Gossip Girl,"
I've been trying to figure out who u r since u started this page. It doesn't seem like u would talk about colleges that much unless u were a senior. I'm only a junior, but I hang out with all the cool seniors. So maybe u r not as cool as u think u r. I still think you might be a perverted gym teacher or somebody like that.
—jdwack

Dearest jdwack,
Get over trying to figure out who I am, because I'm not going to tell you. I will promise you this, though: I would not be caught dead wearing khaki shorts and a whistle around my neck.
—GG

Hey GG,
So what do you think about this big rumor going around that **Flow** and **S** are engaged?? She always acts mysterious, like she's got some big secret, so it's kind of hard to know.
—ghost

Dear ghost,
I know what you mean—**S** is keeping awfully quiet about **Flow**, if the rumor is true. Let's be realistic here, tho. She's only seventeen. Even if they are engaged, I doubt the wedding's just around the corner.
—GG

Hey GossipG,
I don't know if **B** knows this, but I heard that dude she was all

over on Saturday night—her stepbrother's drummer friend—is going to St. Barts for break, too.
—informer

Dear informer,
Yikes. I think **B** is in for a big surprise, and she may not be too pleased about it, either.
—GG

And finally...

Hello? What is the point of being in school after midterms if our grades don't count for anything?? They should just let us take one class, like lunch or study hall or drama, for all of spring term. I mean, it's not like we haven't earned a break!

You know you love me,

gossip girl

barneys builds character

On the Thursday before Christmas, Constance Billard finally released its girls for twelve luxurious days of midterm break. After school, Jenny met Nate in front of Barneys. She was wearing a baby blue cowl-neck sweater, a black parka with a faux fur collar, her supershort gray school uniform, a little red mohair hat with her dark curls poking out from underneath it, and matching red mohair gloves. She looked adorable, and the minute Nate saw her, he took her gloved hand and kissed it on the palm. He had just scored an enormous Christmas surplus of weed from his supplier at the pizza place on Eightieth and Madison, and he was in a very good mood.

"I missed you," he said, his emerald green eyes sparkling in the winter twilight.

Jenny's heart turned immediately to goo. "I missed you, too," she replied, her cheeks a delicate rosy pink. She pulled the Christmas card she'd made for him out of her parka pocket. "Here."

Nate tore open the handmade envelope. He stared at the picture she'd drawn on it in charcoal, watercolors, and gold pen, trying to figure out what it was exactly.

"It's a snowman hugging a reindeer," Jenny explained. "I sort of combined the styles of Matisse and Picasso, but I don't know if it works."

Nate didn't know anything about Matisse or Picasso. He opened the card. *MERRY CHRISTMAS NATE!* it said in glittery gold capital letters. *Love, Jennifer.* Nate smiled and stuffed the card into his coat pocket. "Thanks."

Jenny slipped her arm through his and led him inside the store. "So what do you want for Christmas? I'm buying your present first."

She'd borrowed another fifty dollars from her dad, which was really nothing on top of all the money she already owed him. Jenny had spent more money since she'd been going out with Nate than she had in her whole lifetime.

As any girl will tell you, looking good is expensive, but so, so worth it.

Inside the men's department, Nate handed her a pair of gray merino wool socks. "What about these?"

"Socks? But I want to get you something special. Something with . . . *spirit,*" Jenny insisted. *Panache* was the word she was trying to think of. *Panache.* She'd seen it used in *Vogue,* and it sounded so French and sophisticated.

Nate put the socks back and glanced around the store. "I just don't want you to spend too much money on me, Jennifer."

Jenny beamed back at him, loving him more than ever now. She loved the way he called her Jennifer. She loved the cute little text messages he sent to her cell phone. She loved his wavy golden brown hair and his always tanned, perfect skin. She loved how he did things like kiss her hand. And best of all, she loved how with only a few words in his sexy voice he could make her feel like the luckiest girl in all of Barneys, and that was really saying something.

"It can't just be *socks*," she insisted. "It has to be special."

"Fine," Nate replied with an amused shrug. It was kind of cute that Jenny wanted to buy him something more meaningful than just socks or cologne. She was so genuinely generous and never expected anything in return.

"These?" Jenny held up a pair of red paisley printed flannel shorts with a drawstring. "I think they're supposed to be pajamas."

Nate frowned. "They're a little gay," he said.

Jenny put the shorts back on the rack. "You're right. Sorry." Then she saw a table with stacks of boxer shorts with photo images silk-screened across the butt. There was a pair of bright blue boxer shorts with a red sailboat silk-screened on them. How perfect. Sailing was Nate's thing. He even built sailboats up in Maine. The boxers cost sixty dollars, which was more than she'd anticipated spending and kind of a lot for underwear, but Jenny was willing to forgo an extra ten dollars for the boy she loved more than anyone or anything else in the world.

"Those are pretty cool," said Nate, holding up the boxers and examining the sailboat. "It's not like anyone will be able to see them, though."

A red flush crept up Jenny's neck at the thought of seeing Nate in his underwear. "No, but you have to have them," she insisted. "They're so totally you."

She folded up the boxers and brought them to the counter. "Can you gift wrap these, please?" She turned to Nate. "It's more fun if you get to open them like a real present." Her brown eyes gleamed with excitement. She had a gorgeous boyfriend, she'd bought him a very cool present, and he was smiling at her in that way that made her feel like screaming, *I am SO HAPPY!* She handed Nate the little black Barneys bag. "Happy Hanukkah," she said playfully, even though she was only half Jewish and Nate wasn't Jewish at all.

"Thanks, Jennifer." Nate hadn't expected to find something he really liked, but he thought the boxers were actually kind of groovy. He took her hand. "Now I get to buy you something," he said. "Come on."

He whisked her into the elevator and up to the sixth floor. Jenny didn't know where they were going until the doors opened and they stepped out into the women's lingerie department.

She hesitated. She'd imagined Nate would buy her something Christmassy and cute, like a scarf with a goofy reindeer on it or something. Not *lingerie*.

"Pick out anything you want," Nate said.

Jenny looked around at the racks of flimsy handmade imported lingerie, her face hot with embarrassment. She always bought Bali bras at Macy's because they had extra support and extra-thick straps to keep the weight of her stupendous boobs from making welts in her shoulders. The bras in Barneys looked like they would shred if she put only one boob into them, let alone two. There was no way she was going to pick out a bra or a bustier or even a nightie. First of all, she would absolutely die if Nate found out her actual cup size. Second of all, they probably didn't even make pretty, lacy things like these in her actual cup size.

Jenny wished she could tell Nate she didn't really want any lingerie, but she didn't want to hurt his feelings. Instead, she reached for a simple pair of white La Perla silk panties with pretty pink stitching at the hem and a pink satin bow on the elastic. "These are nice."

"Would you like the matching bra for that?" a salesclerk in her seventies croaked, tottering over to help.

"No," Jenny practically shouted. She yanked the panties

off the hanger and hurried up to the counter so Nate could pay for them and they could get the hell out of there.

The clerk at the register took the panties and began to wrap them in tissue paper. "Just the thong, miss?" she said.

Jenny stared at the piece of white silk hanging from the woman's hands. She could see now that the butt area was basically missing.

She couldn't bear to look at Nate. "Yes," she squeaked. "That's all."

"And we'd like it gift wrapped, please," Nate added. Blair had worn thongs all the time. He didn't see why Jenny was blushing so much.

When the bag was ready, Nate handed it to Jenny and kissed her on the cheek. "Merry Christmas."

Jenny raised her eyes from where she'd been staring fixedly at a piece of fuzz on the cream-colored carpet and took the shopping bag. Here was another thing she loved about Nate—he didn't freak out over things like thongs. He was always calm and cool.

Well, it's kind of hard not to be calm when you're stoned most of the time.

As they rode down in the elevator, Jenny wondered what they were supposed to do now. Go home and model their gifts for each other? Just the thought of walking around in front of Nate with her butt cheeks exposed made her want to die.

The elevator door opened. "I was thinking we could walk over to the St. Regis," Nate said as they walked through the cosmetics department on the way out of the store.

Jenny's heart thumped erratically in her chest. The St. Regis was a hotel. Oh *God*.

"There's a good little bar there. We could have a hot chocolate or something," Nate added.

It sounded like he genuinely wanted hot chocolate, not a peep show in a hotel room. Jenny let out a relieved sigh. "That sounds really good."

But before they reached the exit door, Nate saw two girls, one with pale blond hair pulled up in a ponytail and one with brown hair that hung down her back. It was Serena and Blair, standing at the Estée Lauder counter directly in their path.

Nate put his arm around Jenny and started to steer her in the opposite direction, back into the men's store and out a different exit. It wasn't that he minded being seen with her. It was just easier if they didn't have to talk to anyone, especially Blair.

Jenny hesitated and frowned up at him. "Wait. Where are we going?" she asked, confused.

"Um, I thought maybe I should get a new belt on the way out," Nate said, hoping Blair and Serena hadn't spotted them yet.

Too late.

"Nate?" he heard Serena's voice behind him. "Hey, Natie!"

He turned around slowly. Serena's earthy-sweet sandalwood and lily scent was already filling his nostrils as she threw her arms around him. She released him and kissed Jenny on the cheek. "So, what'd you guys get?"

Jenny blushed again. "Um, nothing really."

Blair was standing a little bit away from them, silently critiquing Jenny's ugly black parka and fuzzy red hat. Nate smiled at her. "Hey, Blair."

Blair hitched her purple Prada tote bag up on her shoulder and shook her hair away from her face. "Hey," she said to no one in particular. She glanced briefly at Jenny. "Hi, Ginny. Merry Christmas."

Jenny held her little Barneys bag behind her back, as if she were afraid Blair might grab it from her and demand to see what was inside. "Merry Christmas," she said weakly.

Blair was so irritated by the sight of them Christmas shopping together like such a boring, happy couple that she couldn't resist fucking with them.

"Maybe you guys can help us," she said, sounding suddenly perky. "We're buying presents for Flow and Miles—you know, the guys we were with the other night? But we aren't sure what to get." She nudged Serena's elbow. "Serena was thinking maybe cologne. Nate, do you mind if we test some on you?"

Nate didn't wear cologne and he really just wanted to get the hell out of there, but he didn't have enough brainpower to extract himself from the situation. "Sure," he replied unenthusiastically.

Blair led them over to a counter and, before he could protest, grabbed Nate's right hand and sprayed it with Dolce & Gabbana cologne that she knew smelled like moldy blue cheese and ass.

"What do you think?" she asked, shoving Nate's hand under Jenny's nose.

Jenny started to sneeze.

"Bless you," Serena said.

Jenny sneezed and sneezed. She couldn't stop.

Nate winced. "It's a little strong."

"Really? What about this, then?" Blair grabbed his left hand and sprayed it with Hermès Eau D'Orange Verte. It was a clean, classic scent that she loved so much, she wore it sometimes herself, even though it was for men.

Nate sniffed his hand and was instantly overcome with nostalgia, thinking back to the days when he would lie on Blair's bed, kissing her bare stomach and making her laugh.

"Nice," he said, taking another whiff.

Jenny's nose was running. She wiped it on her glove.

Serena picked up Nate's left hand and held it under her nose. "Oh, that's so totally you, Nate." She smiled sincerely at Jenny. "You should buy him some of this for Christmas. It's awesome."

Jenny wiped her nose again. She didn't have any money left and besides, she'd already bought Nate a much better present. She glanced at Nate, hoping he would say as much and then they could go, but Nate just stood there staring at Blair with his hands outstretched like some kind of dumb cologne model.

Doubt nudged its way back into Jenny's heart. How come Nate was so wonderful when she was alone with him, but when they were around other people he acted so . . . *stupid?*

Blair wrinkled her nose. "I don't know," she mused. "I think maybe we should give them something more personal."

"Like what, though?" Serena asked, getting in on the game.

"I just bought Nate a really neat pair of boxers with a sailboat silk-screened on them," Jenny suggested helpfully. "They've got all different ones. You should go and see."

Nate grinned sheepishly. "Yeah. They're pretty cool."

Blair gripped the green sample bottle of Hermès cologne, ready to hurl it at Jenny's head. *Boxers?* The little whore.

Serena could see that Blair's little prank seemed to be backfiring on her. "Come on, Blair." She tugged gently on Blair's elbow. "Let's go upstairs. There's a bikini I want to try on. You can tell me what you think."

Blair put the cologne bottle back down on the counter. "Fine," she retorted coolly.

"We're going to St. Barts tomorrow." Serena planted a kiss on Nate's cheek. Then she bent down and kissed Jenny. "But we'll see you at New Year's, okay?"

Nate watched Blair fiddle with the ruby ring on her finger.

He took a step forward, put his hand on her coat sleeve, and kissed her on the cheek. "Merry Christmas, Blair."

The best actresses always remain composed in the face of insult.

"Merry Christmas," she replied, keeping her chin raised as high as was physically possible without falling over backward. Then, with as much poise as she could muster, she turned toward the bank of elevators in the back of the store, pulling Serena along after her.

Nate watched them go, admiring the way Blair's long dark hair hung down the back of her sky-blue cashmere coat. He raised his left hand and breathed in that clean, fresh scent that reminded him of Blair's bare skin. Then he turned back to Jenny. Her dark puff of curls. Her bulky black parka. Her itsy-bitsy hands. Her shy smile. It was a relief to have Blair gone so he could stop comparing them. Because the honest truth was, there was no comparison.

A perfume bottle in the shape of a ballet dancer stood on the glass counter beside them.

"Hey," Nate changed the subject. "Have you ever seen the *Nutcracker*?" Jenny was into art, so she probably knew all about ballet.

Jenny shook her head, smiling tentatively. She'd been to Lincoln Center with her architecture and design class, but that was as close as she'd come to seeing a real ballet. "No, not yet."

That wouldn't do. That definitely wouldn't do. Nate had taken Blair to the *Nutcracker* for the past three Christmases, and even though he knew it was seriously uncool, he always really enjoyed it. It was such a trip the way in the first scene, during the Christmas party, the tree on stage was just a normal, average-size tree. Then, after the little girl went to sleep and started to dream, the tree grew out of the floor, turning into this humongous tree on steroids—way bigger, even, than the tree in Rockefeller Center. And then all the toys came to life and started fighting with one another. It was awesome.

Nate pulled his cell phone out of his pocket. "We're having dinner at your dad's tomorrow night, right?"

Jenny nodded.

"Then let's see if they have any tickets left for the matinee."

Jenny leaned back against the perfume counter, overcome by those flulike symptoms again. Nate was taking her to the ballet! How could she *not* love him?

d tries to write about sex in a new way

As soon as his last midterm was over on Thursday, Dan walked to his favorite Chinese-Cuban coffee shop on Broadway and ordered a café con leche and an egg roll. Then he got out a brand-new black notebook and a black ballpoint pen. All week long he'd been trying to write something halfway decent to send with his college applications, but everything he wrote was complete garbage. He'd never had trouble writing before—usually the words just flowed out of him. Sure, he'd been distracted by midterms, but there was still no denying it. He had writer's block.

Dan sipped his coffee, dribbling milky brown drops all over the first clean white page in his notebook. In a way, having writer's block put him in league with the big boys. Tolstoy had it, Hemingway had it. He wasn't sure if any of his favorite French existentialist writers had it, but then he figured they probably all must have at one time or another. That didn't make it any less painful, though. In fact, it was excruciating.

Poor, tormented soul.

Dan could tell from looking at his old black notebooks that the last time he'd written anything worth saving was before Thanksgiving, before he and Vanessa had kissed for the first time and realized they were in love.

He rolled his egg roll around in sticky plum sauce and took a bite. Aside from death, love was his favorite topic, but now that he was *in* love, the words he used to write about it all seemed so superficial and clumsy. If he could only find some new angle from which to approach the topic of love. He dipped the egg roll in sauce and bit into it again. Hot egg roll grease ran down his wrist. A waitress bumped his elbow with her hip and he dropped what remained of the egg roll into his mug, spattering milky coffee everywhere.

Most people would have been pissed, but for Dan it was a lightbulb moment.

Sex! he thought. Sex was the ultimate physical expression of love, which was why, when he ever actually did it, he wanted it to be at the moment when the only way to say what he truly wanted to say was to make love.

Dan uncapped his pen. He'd read enough critical theory to know that some of the most clichéd ways to write about sex were using images of blooming flowers, sunrises, and fireworks. He also knew it was possible to make just about anything sound sexual. But he wanted to write about sex in new and unexpected ways.

He stared at the half-eaten egg roll marooned in his coffee, thinking.

Any normal boy thinking about sex would have instantly thought about taking his girlfriend's clothes off. However, Dan wasn't a normal boy. Instead of thinking about taking Vanessa's clothes off, he was thinking about words, and the fact is, there's nothing sexy about plain old words unless they're being used in a sexy way. And in order to do that, you have to stop thinking about words and start thinking about something, or, even better, some*body* else. Preferably with their clothes off.

But Dan was stuck on the words. The more he agonized over which words to use, the more convinced he became that he couldn't write about sex because he hadn't had it yet. And if he couldn't write about sex, he couldn't write about love, and if he couldn't write about love, he couldn't write about anything at all.

Was sex the cure for writer's block?

v discovers victoria's secret

After school on Thursday, Vanessa was walking down Broadway in Soho filming a transvestite dressed in a black PVC jumpsuit and six-inch black PVC platform boots walking a tiny black Chihuahua in a fuzzy orange sweater when she was stopped in front of Victoria's Secret by a woman handing out promotional flyers introducing the Very Sexy lingerie collection.

Buy two Very Sexy bras and get a free matching v-string or tanga! the flyer said.

Vanessa wasn't sure what a v-string or a tanga was. She bought her Hanes Her Way cotton underwear and tank tops at Rite Aid and had never even been inside a Victoria's Secret before. She looked up at the posters of Gisele Bündchen modeling the Angels collection that filled the windows. *Seamless lingerie with a heavenly fit*, the posters read. Of course anything would look seamless and heavenly on Gisele, but would it look good on *her?*

Vanessa slung her camera strap over her shoulder and pulled open the store's heavy glass door, thinking it might be kind of amusing to find out.

She was accosted as soon as the door swung shut behind her.

"Welcome to Victoria's Secret," said a petite blond woman in a tight black pantsuit. "Can I help you find anything today?"

Vanessa glared at her. She hated hovering salespeople. "No," she said dismissively. "I'm just looking."

The woman smiled graciously. "That's fine. Just so you know, my name is Vanessa."

Vanessa stared at her in surprise. "That's my name, too," she said, feeling sort of bad that she'd been so rude to the woman. "We have the same name."

Blond Vanessa beamed back at her. "Isn't that a coincidence? Well, you won't forget my name. Just give me a holler if you need anything." Then she turned away to help another customer.

Vanessa glanced around the store. Perfume and chamber music filled the air, and the carpet on the floor was a deep, velvety red. Round tables draped with red satin were stacked with thongs and panties in solids, animal prints, and floral patterns. On every wall hung racks of bras in lace, stretch satin, and cotton. There were teddies, tangas, v-strings, and boy shorts. Slips, bustiers, garters, and garter belts.

Vanessa had never seen so much square footage devoted to the type of girly vanity she had always loathed. But maybe, just maybe, a Very Sexy rose lace plunge demi bra and matching lace tanga were just the type of thing she needed to make herself so irresistible to Dan, he'd have his organic poetic moment or whatever it was he was waiting for and decide he was ready to have sex.

She walked over to a rack of red lace underwire bras and flicked through them. Thirty-four B, 36C, 38D. She didn't even know what size she was. Beneath the rack of bras was a rack of lacy underwear, more like lace shorts than panties—*extremely* short shorts. Vanessa examined the tags. So *these* were tangas. Well, they didn't look so bad. She glanced around the room, searching for her blond namesake.

"Decided you'd like to try something on after all?" Blond Vanessa asked, stepping around a counter to Vanessa's left, where she'd been busy folding a stack of white cotton thongs.

Vanessa shrugged helplessly. "Um, does this come in black?" She held up one of the red lace Very Sexy demi bras.

"What size do you need?" asked Blond Vanessa.

Vanessa frowned. How could she have gotten through seventeen years of life without knowing her own bra size? "I'm not sure," she mumbled almost inaudibly.

Blond Vanessa smiled benevolently. "Let's find a changing room, then, and I'll measure you. Then we can talk about what you're looking for. We'll find something in a style you like that suits your figure and is comfortable to wear, too! How does that sound?"

Vanessa nodded reluctantly. She didn't exactly like the idea of someone measuring her chest, and she had no clue what she was looking for, but Blond Vanessa seemed like a pro, and she had already come this far so she might as well go for it. "As long as it comes in black," she insisted.

We know, we know.

Disclaimer: All the real names of places, people, and events have been altered or abbreviated to protect the innocent. Namely, me.

hey people!

Love your sister, but not too much

It's come to my attention that we haven't heard a peep out of **B**'s adorable dreadlocked stepbrother, **A**, lately. You might think he's too busy studying for exams and getting his new band together. But no. He's *hiding*. And I'm almost convinced that the reason he's hiding is because he's dealing with some serious issues. Well, one issue, to be exact: He's in love with his stepsister. The latest is that he's invited his drum-playing friend **M** along to St. Barts with him, and I suspect that the reason he's done it is so **M** will keep **B** occupied and out of his sight.

Your e-mail

Dear GG,
I'm in **J**'s health class, and I know for a fact that she's in therapy for this condition where she's obsessed with belly buttons. She, like, has to go to the bathroom every hour to make sure hers is still there, and when we're changing for gym she always stares at everybody else's. It's really freaky.
—ronisays

A: Hey ronisays,
So, what's wrong with that? Belly buttons are sexy. At least, *mine* is.
—GG

Hey GG,
Just thought you'd like to know that I think I live in the same building as the **B** you're always talking about and sometimes I get her mail by mistake. Her mom gets tons of mail from New

Beginnings, which is either a fertility clinic or a drug and alcohol counseling center. I looked it up in the phone book.
—peekaboo

Hi peekaboo,
Let's hope she just gives them money and doesn't actually use their services!
—GG

Sightings

S giving her doorman a three-foot-tall solid chocolate snowman wrapped in **Godiva**'s signature gold leaf. *Flow* really is going overboard, unless **S** has some other admirer—she throws the little gift cards away without reading them. **D** staring into the water down by the Seventy-ninth Street boat basin, looking for inspiration. **V** in a bar in Billyburg, trying out her new **Victoria's Secret**-enhanced figure, perhaps? **B** and **S** leaving the **J. Sisters** Salon after their pre-St. Barts bikini waxes.

Looks like it's going to be hotter than hot down there!

Have an amazing vacation and don't forget to have as much crazy fun as possible. I know I will. See you out there!

You know you love me,

gossip girl

b is stuck in economy class, drawing guys like flies

Blair Waldorf   Yale University Application Essay   December 23

The thing I love most about Audrey Hepburn's film persona is that she's aloof and approachable at the same time. She's poised, but down-to-earth. She's mysterious, but open.

Blair stopped typing and pressed the backspace button on her iBook until all the words had been erased. *Film persona?* What the hell was that? It made her sound like some poseur film freak like Vanessa Abrams, that girl in her film class with the shaved head and fat knees. The thing was, Blair had to write about Audrey Hepburn as she appeared in her films and not as a real person, because Blair honestly didn't know all that much about the real Audrey other than that she'd stopped dressing in custom-made Givenchy couture when she got older, cut all her hair off, and just wore khakis and black turtlenecks all the time. Blair had taken out a bunch of books on Audrey Hepburn from the library but never got past the first chapter. She didn't really want to hear about Audrey's colitis problem or her work with UNICEF. It was so much more interesting to *imagine* what

Audrey's life had been like than to read the real facts.

"What're you writing?" Miles asked, refreshing her orange juice with a minibottle of Smirnoff vodka.

As it turned out, Aaron had invited Miles to St. Barts to spend Christmas with them and decided not to tell Blair about it until they met up at the United Airlines check-in desk. It was pretty obvious that the only reason Miles had come was because he thought he'd spend the entire trip getting it on with Blair. But Blair was determined to make him see before they even landed that he was sadly mistaken.

"Nothing," she said without looking up.

They'd had to leave the apartment at the ungodly hour of seven-forty in the morning. Now it was one o'clock and the plane was still an hour away from St. Barts. Aaron was asleep—or maybe he was just pretending to be asleep so he wouldn't have to watch Miles hitting on Blair. Serena was listening to Coldplay on her Discman, relieved to be away from Flow's constant flood of gifts. Tyler was playing chess on his Game Boy and sulking because at the last minute his friend Prince Rolf von Wurtzel's mother had decided not to let Rolf come to St. Barts with Tyler because the young German prince had an embarrassing bed-wetting problem. Blair stirred the ice cubes around in her drink with a little brown plastic straw. Thank fucking God for small favors.

"I tried to call you all week," Miles told her as he reclined his seat in an attempt to stretch his long legs out in front of him. Much to Blair's consternation, they were all packed into economy class like sardines. "But I must have written your number down wrong or something."

Blair kept her eyes on her computer screen. *No,* she replied silently. *I just gave you a fake number.*

Miles reached up and skimmed his fingers along the ends of Blair's long hair. "I missed you," he whispered.

She glanced at him, unsmiling, and then looked away again, wondering what Audrey Hepburn would do in such an unpleasant situation.

You know those religious wackjobs who have bumper stickers on their cars that say, "What would Jesus do?" Well, Blair had a similar saying: "What would Audrey do?"

It wasn't that she had anything against Miles. He wasn't a slimeball, and he wore amazing Armani clothes. He was nice looking and he was friends with Aaron, who was also an okay guy, although if she had her preference, she wouldn't have a stepbrother at all. Blair should have felt flattered by Miles's attention, and maybe she would have if she'd been in the mood to flirt with him. But the reality was that at eleven o'clock in the morning, crammed into economy class on a crummy little airplane with her computer in her lap and her dirty hair in a ponytail, she didn't feel like flirting with anyone.

"Excuse me, miss, would you be interested in a copy of British *Vogue*?" the steward from first class asked. He looked like a younger, taller Pierce Brosnan, and if he hadn't been wearing a United Airlines uniform, he might even have been hot.

Blair took the magazine. She noticed that the steward wasn't passing out British *Vogue*s to everyone in economy, only to her.

"Can I get you a drink? Champagne?" he offered with a wink.

Blair dropped the magazine on the floor. Couldn't he tell she was busy? "No, thank you," she replied.

Miles handed the steward his empty rum-and-Coke glass. "I'll take another one."

The steward took the glass, looking annoyed that he'd specifically asked Blair if she wanted something and now he was stuck waiting on the teenage hotshot sitting next to her. Miles went back to stroking the ends of her hair. "Aren't you going to read your magazine?"

Blair wanted to tell him to go shove the magazine up his Armani ass, but she knew that in such a situation Audrey would remain calm and continue to do what she was doing in hopes that the offending person would get the hint and leave her alone.

She turned her attention back to her essay. What she wanted to say was that Audrey had all the qualities Blair thought a woman ought to have. Style, beauty, grace, intelligence, wit, courage, and a certain mystery that made men fall for her instantly. But Blair wasn't an idiot. She couldn't very well say in her Yale application essay that the reason she admired Audrey Hepburn was that she was irresistible to men—especially not after Blair had kissed her interviewer.

Ms. Glos had told her not to be so literal. Blair arranged her fingers on the keyboard again and started to type, letting the words flow without really planning what she was going to say.

Sometimes I dream that I am Audrey Hepburn. I feel lighter and clearer and I speak with the same cool accent she had. Audrey made everything look easy. She never had to take AP exams or rewrite a stupid college application essay. She never had to go on vacation with her mom or her fat, annoying stepfather or her stepbrother's annoying, horny friend. Her boyfriend never ditched her for a ten-year-old. And even if she did have problems, she kept quiet about them and dealt with them on her own instead of telling everyone in the world, including her interviewer at Yale. When I am Audrey, I feel like I can take on the world.

Blair reread what she had written and then blacked out the whole paragraph and deleted it. *When I am Audrey I am psycho* was more like it.

"And it looks like a beautiful day in the area as we begin our descent into St. Barts," the captain's deep voice came on over the plane's sound system. "I'd just like to take this time to thank you for flying with us today. I'd especially like to thank the cute brunette in 24 B. Have a great vacation, and I hope you'll choose United again whenever you fly."

Twenty-four B. Blair looked up at the little tag on the ceiling. That was her seat. Had she only *imagined* the pilot had just hit on her, or had he actually done it?

Miles was still stroking her hair. The steward came back with Miles's drink and a glass of champagne for Blair, even though she'd said she didn't want one.

"Compliments of the pilot," the steward said with a knowing smile.

Blair felt like Mia Farrow in *Alice,* the Woody Allen movie that Mr. Beckham had made her film class watch not once but twice. In the movie, Alice—this dull Park Avenue mom—had gone to some weird place in Chinatown where she ate these funky Chinese herbs that attracted guys to her like flies.

Not one to refuse a drink when it was handed to her, Blair downed the glass of champagne and snapped her laptop closed, dumping it into her Louis Vuitton carry-on bag and kicking it under the seat in front of her. The plane was beginning to descend, and outside the window the warm Caribbean Sea glittered promisingly. Blair twisted her ruby ring around and around on her finger, eager to get into her new black Gucci bikini and out onto the beach, away from everyone and everything.

Aaron opened his eyes and sat up, blocking her view. He smiled at her. "Finish your essay?"

"Fuck off," Blair answered.

d is ready, or not

"More curry powder!" Rufus Humphrey growled at the tomato sauce after he tasted it. "More rum!" It was Friday afternoon and his annual holiday bash was due to kick off in an hour.

"But Dad, isn't lasagna supposed to taste Italian?" argued Dan.

His father furrowed his bushy gray eyebrows and wiped his sauce-smeared hands on his dirty white SAVE THE COMMIES! T-shirt. "When did you become such a tight-ass?" He waved a wooden spoon above his head. "There are no rules here, only possibilities!"

Dan shrugged and poured a few cups of dark rum into the sauce. No wonder everyone always raved about his dad's lasagna. After a few bites they were completely wasted.

"So who's this dude your sister has invited?" Rufus asked. He used words like *dude* to mock the way Dan and Jenny talked. It was completely annoying.

"His name is Nate," Dan said distractedly. "He's pretty cool," he added, although he was pretty sure his dad would actually despise Nate. Nate wore polo shirts and had an expensive haircut. He wore leather shoes and a leather belt, and he was usually so baked, he couldn't have a conversation without breaking into an asinine giggle in the middle of it. But Dan didn't bother explaining this to his dad. He was too distracted by the fact that Vanessa was going to arrive any minute and he'd almost made up his mind that he was going to tell her he wanted to have sex.

"Well, let's hope this Nate person likes Lasagna Punjabi," Rufus quipped, filling his oversized Mets coffee mug with Chianti.

The doorbell rang and Rufus dashed over to let in his oldest friend, Lyle Gross, whom he had met in the park twenty years ago. Lyle was one of those ageless guys you always saw sitting on a park bench, listening to a Mets game on a handheld radio and studying a *Daily News* from three weeks ago that he'd found in the trash. He was a writer, he said, although Dan had never seen any proof of this.

"I brought grapes," announced Lyle. He'd combed his thin gray hair over his bald spot and was wearing a mustard-yellow sweater, maroon wool pants, and white Nike tennis shoes. There were little scabs all over his neck where he'd nicked himself shaving. It was kind of hard to look at him. "Hello, Danielson!"

"Hi," Dan said back. Lyle was always adding little flourishes to people's names. He probably thought it was hilariously funny, but Dan didn't see the humor in it.

Rufus grabbed the grapes and tossed them to Dan. "Throw some of these in, too," he ordered.

"Okay." Dubiously, Dan pulled a few grapes off the stem and dropped them into the sauce. At this point he could drop one of Marx's turds in there and no one would notice. Marx was their very overweight tabby cat who was now lying sprawled out on the kitchen table between a baguette and a huge wheel of parmesan cheese.

While Rufus and Lyle were in the living room choosing a record from Rufus's old vinyl collection, Dan stirred the sauce with a trembling hand, wondering exactly how he should broach the topic of sex to Vanessa. He'd told her he wanted it to be organic, but who was he kidding? Now all he really wanted was to get it over with *fast* so he could get back to writing because he was sick and tired of staring at his little black notebooks with his mind as blank and empty as the page.

Dan stirred the sauce faster and faster, until red tomato goo oozed over the sides of the pan. He'd just have to come out and say it, and hopefully Vanessa wouldn't laugh at him.

v is in the right place at the wrong time

Vanessa was supposed to be at Dan's house already, but she had lugged all her film equipment along with her, and it was such a haul—first the L train from Williamsburg to West Fourteenth and then the E train up to the edge of Central Park—and it was such a beautiful evening, it would be a shame not to get any footage for her film essay while she was out. It had snowed last night and the walkways in the park were frozen and slippery. As she tromped down the path to the frozen lake, Vanessa wished she'd thrown her new Victoria's Secret underwear into her bag instead of wearing it under her clothes. The lace felt cold against her skin and was chafing her in all the wrong places.

Beside the pond was a huge old oak tree, its branches dripping with icicles. Vanessa pulled her camera out of its case. She could shoot the icicles and use them in the opening credits to her New York film essay. What a cool way to introduce the setting. For a moment, people would think the film was set in the serene countryside. Then she would cut to something distinctly urban, like meat packers unloading bloody carcasses down on West Street.

She fiddled with the lens, trying to come in close on the

icicles and then panning back. It felt a little too *National Geographic* to do it the other way around. Dan was always telling her she needed to get more action into her films, but Vanessa insisted that film was exactly like poetry. Nothing necessarily had to happen; you just had to feel something.

And as Vanessa stood in the snow at the edge of the frozen pond trying to capture the icicles' stark, momentary beauty, she was definitely feeling something: the sensation of a black lace tanga freeze-branding itself on her ass.

Earlier that afternoon, Nate had taken Jenny to see the matinee of the *Nutcracker* at Lincoln Center. It was just as Nate had remembered it, with the humongous Christmas tree and the awesome life-size fighting mice. Jenny had sat in wonder, enthralled by the music, the scenery, the dancers, and the costumes—especially the Sugarplum Fairy. Her heart was full to bursting in the end when Clara and her Nutcracker Prince sailed into the sky in their horse-drawn sled.

Afterward, Jenny and Nate had been supposed to head straight up to her house for Rufus's dinner party, but there was no quicker way to kill a perfect afternoon than by walking in on her father with his shirt off in the kitchen pouring rum and a giant economy-size bottle of ketchup into a pot. Nate had been *so perfect* all day, holding her hand and pointing out his favorite parts in the ballet. He even *looked* perfect in his gray cashmere suit and periwinkle blue shirt. So instead Jenny decided to go home the long way, via Central Park.

As they headed down the path to the boat pond, she reached for Nate's hand and held on tight. Her black suede boots had smooth soles and kept slipping on the ice. Now that she was no longer distracted by the ballet, she couldn't help but notice the weird chafing feeling in her butt crack.

Silently she reminded herself to relax—she didn't have a major wedgie, she was just wearing her new thong.

Nate's free hand was clasped around the Ziploc bag of weed in his wool coat pocket, keeping it warm. There was nothing worse than frozen weed. It got all soggy and smoked like hell when you lit it. He'd meant to light up as soon as they got out of the ballet, but there was something surreal and beautiful about the sun sinking into the snow and the warmth of Jenny's hand in his that made him not feel like bothering with a joint. He just felt like talking.

"It sucks I have to go up to Maine tomorrow," he said. "But I have to get my applications done, so it's good I'll be someplace quiet. My interviewer at Brown said they have this cool new major called Science and Technology Studies. I was thinking if I go there, I could maybe design boats as part of my major, you know?"

Jenny nodded, concentrating on her feet. She didn't want Nate to go away tomorrow. She didn't want him to go away to college, either.

The lake was in sight now. In the spring, Nate liked to stand in the gazebo, get high, and watch the ducks and their little ducklings swimming around. The lake would be totally frozen now. Maybe they could even walk on it.

"It's weird," he continued. "This time last year I knew exactly where I'd be in one year: here, in the city, going to school and fucking around with my friends, the same as always. But I have no idea where I'll be next year. It's crazy."

Jenny turned to look at Nate, wondering how he'd react if she told him she loved him right now. His cheeks were pink from the cold and so were the tips of his adorable, perfect ears. He was so gorgeous, she felt like screaming every time she looked at him.

"I'm wearing the thong," she breathed before she could stop herself. She started walking faster. She couldn't believe she'd said it!

"Wait. What?" Nate quickened his pace in order to keep up with her. He hadn't even heard what she'd said.

Jenny let go of his hand. "I'm wearing the thong!" she exclaimed, a little louder this time. Then she giggled and broke into a run, slipping and sliding down the hill to the frozen pond.

Nate heard her that time. He released his grip on the Ziploc baggie and started to chase after her. "Come back here! I vant to see zat thong!" he shouted in a scary vampire voice.

Jenny squealed and kept running. Her eyes were streaming from the cold and her breath caught in her throat.

Nate chased her all the way out onto the snow-covered ice, where Jenny's feet slipped out from underneath her, sending her sprawling beneath a big oak tree adorned with long, crystalline icicles. He dive-bombed on top of her, and they rolled around, giggling breathlessly and getting snow in their hair.

Nate turned Jenny over on her stomach and pulled up her coat. "Let me see, let me see!" he cried, grappling with the back of her black velvet pants and pulling them down to get a glimpse of her bare ass.

"Wait!" Jenny squealed, giggling and squirming. She squeezed her eyes shut, unable to hold back any longer. "Wait. Nate, *I love you!*"

Nate paused for a moment, absorbing the information. Then, instead of turning her around and kissing her and telling her he loved her, too, he blew a raspberry on the top of one of her cute pink butt cheeks and then flopped over on his back, breathing clouds of warm air up into the cold blue sky.

Jenny stayed sprawled out on her stomach for a few more

seconds, catching her breath. Then she pushed herself up to standing and readjusted her clothes. She was glad she'd finally said it, but it would have been a lot nicer if Nate had said it right back. He was supposed to say, "I love you," and then pick her up and carry her to a horse-drawn sled to never-never land.

But all Nate had done was make a farting noise on her bare butt.

"You're not wearing your sailboat boxers, are you?" she asked hopefully, trying to maintain the playful note things had started on.

"I'm not sure." Nate reached down and unbuckled his belt. He wriggled his pants down over his hips. "Blue plaid," he said. "Sorry."

"That's okay," Jenny responded quickly, pulling her coat around herself. "Hey," she said, changing the subject. "Let's walk by the Romeo and Juliet statue. It's my favorite, and it's on the way."

Nate spent a lot of time in the park, but he had no idea what she was talking about. "What Romeo and Juliet statue?"

Jenny rubbed her hands up and down the tops of her arms. "Never mind. I'll show you when we get there."

"Are you cold?" Nate asked, sitting up on his elbows and holding out his hand. "Come here."

She hesitated for a second and then walked over. Nate pulled her down on top of him and wrapped her inside his coat, kissing her forehead and then each of her cold, rosy cheeks.

She brushed her lips against his chin and couldn't resist saying it again. Maybe, just maybe, he hadn't heard her the first time.

"I love you," she whispered.

This time Nate had to respond. He was holding her, and

she was looking into his green eyes with her big brown ones, waiting.

And they'd just seen the *Nutcracker*, for God's sake, which was a love story, in case he didn't remember.

"I love you, too," he murmured.

And then they kissed for a long, long time. Jenny's red hat fell off and her dark brown curls fell over their faces, shrouding them.

But not very well.

Dan had told Vanessa her films needed more action. Well, here was definitely some action. Yes, the icicles were great, superb. But how often did you see a woman baring her naked bottom in the snow? How often did you see a totally clean-cut guy pulling down his pants in broad daylight in the middle of winter? And how often did you see a couple rolling around inside the same overcoat in the middle of a frozen pond, in the middle of the busiest city in the world? If only Vanessa had had a helicopter, she would have flown up and up and panned way, way back until the couple was just a pin-speck in the middle of the grid of Manhattan. But she didn't have a helicopter, so she would have to get creative with editing. The best part was that she hadn't zoomed in completely on the couple's faces, so they could be anyone of any age—you and your boyfriend, or your grandma and *her* boyfriend. It was pure poetry, raw and beautiful. She couldn't wait to show Dan.

Wait. Would that be before or after she showed him what she had on under her black turtleneck and black wool skirt?

la isla bonita

The Isle de la Paix resort on the island of St. Barts was the type of place where celebrities go to hide and middle-aged New York society women go to recover from plastic surgery. Unless you were somebody or you knew somebody, you couldn't stay there. But it just so happened that Cyrus Rose, Blair's stepfather, owned the development company that had built the resort, and so the three villas that he and Blair's mother had reserved for the family were the best ones there.

Serena and Blair's villa had a wraparound deck from which they could see the resort's swimming pool, where women over forty with surgically enhanced breasts and surgically reduced thighs lay on chaise lounges wearing huge sunglasses and strapless maillots and pretended to read French fashion magazines while they got extremely drunk on the house rum punch. One of the women had her petite white bichon frise with her, and even the dog was wearing sunglasses. From the other side of the deck they could see the perfect stretch of white-sand beach where the younger women were sunbathing topless and guys sailed nonchalantly by on Windsurfers, pretending not to look. The sea was so calm and such a perfect shade of green-blue that it looked fake.

Serena sat on the porch, smoking a Gitane and flipping through French *Elle*, waiting for Blair to get dressed before they met everyone in the dining room for a late lunch. She'd just washed her hair, and it dripped onto her bare shoulders and down the back of her yellow Diane von Furstenberg halter top. After her shower, she'd rubbed herself all over with Lancôme self-tanning lotion, and her skin had already turned a healthy, golden brown. Her tiny white denim Agnès B. miniskirt barely covered the tops of her legs, and on her feet were a pair of white leather thongs encrusted with crystals.

Near the deck railing, a hummingbird was sucking pollen from a hibiscus bush, flitting from flower to flower. Serena wondered why it didn't just stay on one flower and take a good long drink instead of moving around so much.

Good question.

"Hello? Pardon?" Serena heard a man say with a French accent. She stamped out her cigarette with the sole of her shoe and stood up. A guy wearing an Isle de la Paix T-shirt was standing at the foot of the deck steps holding a huge bouquet of rare tropical flowers. *"Ça c'est pour vous, mademoiselle,"* he announced, carrying the flowers up the steps and handing them to Serena.

Jesus. Did Flow have spies or something? How the hell had he found her?

Serena took the flowers and sniffed them. "Thanks," she told the guy.

"No problem," he replied in English. He was about to turn away when Blair opened the screen door to the villa and came out onto the deck.

"My mom better have an account set up at the bar," she told Serena before she even noticed the guy. Blair was dressed in a beige silk jersey slip dress that was practically the same color as her Lancôme tan. From afar it looked like she was completely naked. On her feet were a pair of red rubber flip-flops she'd bought in the drugstore, and she'd put a fake diamond toe ring on the pinkie toe of her left foot, trying out a new white-trash-with-cash look. She noticed the resort dude staring at her. "Yes?" she demanded. *"Parlezvous Anglais?"*

The guy looked embarrassed. "Sorry. I just wanted to say 'welcome' to the two most beautiful girls on the island."

Luckily, his accent was extremely sexy. It was the only way he could have gotten away with saying something so completely cheesy.

"Thanks," Blair said. "We'll see you later," she added, dismissing him.

"Enjoy the flowers, mademoiselle," the guy said, nodding at Serena. Then he grinned at Blair again and left.

Blair combed her hair with her fingers and squinted out to sea. Getting picked up by every guy she ran into was becoming a tad boring.

Serena put the flowers down on the rattan table in the middle of the deck.

"Who're they from?" Blair asked.

Serena shrugged. "I don't think you have to ask."

Blair walked over and untaped the gift card from the square glass vase the flowers had come in. " 'Have an awesome vacation and don't stress out too much over the wedding plans,' " she read aloud. " 'Love, your dear friends K and I.' "

Blair and Serena looked at each other and burst out laughing.

Serena was actually relieved to discover that maybe Flow hadn't sent all those gifts himself. The chocolate snowman and the fishbowl full of baby barracudas, for instance. Maybe Kati and Isabel had sent those, too.

"Come on," she said, grabbing Blair's arm and pulling her down the villa steps. "Let's go let Cyrus buy us a drink!"

Aaron and Miles were already in the bar playing backgammon and trying to get Tyler to eat fried conch. Blair's mother and Cyrus were still out sailing on some owner's yacht, so no one had seen them yet.

The resort dining room wasn't really a room at all, just a large covered deck facing the beach and the perfectly blue-green sea. To one side of the deck was a bar fashioned from bamboo and glass, with white leather barstools. Very modern tropical chic.

"Two rum and Cokes please," Blair told the bartender in French. The great thing about being on a French island was that you didn't have to worry about getting carded.

Not that she got carded very often.

Serena took her drink and clinked glasses with Blair. "To us," she toasted. And then they both tilted back their heads and chugged.

"Whoa," Miles breathed, watching Blair admiringly. He had changed into black Armani cargo pants and a cement gray Armani polo shirt and looked too pale now that he was out of the city. "How can you do that without burping like a truck driver afterward?"

Blair grinned and wiped her lips with the back of her hand. "Practice."

Aaron shook his head. His dreadlocks looked more appropriate now, with the beach in the background. He shoved his hands in the pockets of his army green cargo shorts. "I'm not sure that's something to be proud of."

Blair rolled her eyes. "As if you never drink."

Aaron shrugged. "I drink. I just prefer to drink water when I'm thirsty."

Tyler took a bite of conch and then spat it into a cocktail napkin. "And Blair drinks rubbing alcohol," he quipped.

Blair was about to smack him, but then she caught sight of her mother and Cyrus walking down the dock toward them. Cyrus was holding onto Eleanor's elbow as if he were concerned she might trip. If it had been anyone else, Blair might have thought that was sweet, but in her opinion nothing Cyrus did was ever sweet. Her mother was wearing a bright green-and-pink Lilly Pulitzer dress with white frogs all over it that would have looked a lot better if it was all one color and covered her not-so-thin legs a little more. Her highlighted blond bob was tucked into a white linen headband, and her face was deeply tanned. Cyrus was wearing red linen pleated pants and a navy-blue-and-white-striped polo shirt. His face was red and shiny, and he couldn't have looked more porcine.

Meaning "piglike," for those who got low scores on their SAT verbal.

Eleanor Waldorf Rose squealed when she saw them all standing at the bar. "Hello, kidlets!" she cried, rushing over and squeezing Tyler tight. She let go of him and threw herself at Blair. "I've missed you so much. And I've got so much to tell you!"

Serena smiled politely. "Hello, Mrs. Rose." Blair's mother was kind of a ditz, but she was a lot less stuck-up than her own mother.

Cyrus shook Aaron's hand. "Glad to see you, son. My lawyer hasn't called me, so I guess you and Blair managed not to burn the building down while we were gone."

Aaron grinned. "Oh, we did. We're building you a new one. You'll see when you get back. It's going to be really cool."

Blair decided to have a little fun, too. Or maybe she was just drunk. "And I got pregnant," she said. She put her arm around Miles. "This is Miles. He's the father."

The grin disappeared from Aaron's face.

"Since when did you become such a comedienne?" Eleanor asked, cocking her head in wonder at her daughter's lewd sense of humor.

Blair removed her arm from Miles's shoulders and flashed her mother a wry smile. "After I dropped out of Constance?"

Serena giggled. "You're such a liar."

Cyrus grabbed Blair with a meaty paw and pulled her into a hug. "Someone's in a good mood!" he said.

Not anymore.

Letting go of Blair, Cyrus signaled to the bartender. "Champagne for everyone!"

Blair winced. Talk about *tacky.*

Eleanor patted her stomach. "Not me, darling."

Since when did she turn down champagne?

"The more for us." Cyrus winked at Blair and passed out glasses to Aaron, Blair, Serena, Miles and Tyler. He handed Eleanor a glass of seltzer and then held his champagne out in front of him. "To our big, happy family," he boomed, grinning like an idiot.

Blair had had enough family time already. "Can we sit down and eat?" she whined. "I'm starving." She hadn't made herself throw up since her mother and Cyrus had been away, but she had a feeling that anything and everything she ate today wasn't going to stay down for very long.

They trooped into the open-air dining room and sat down at one of the white leather banquettes. A ceiling fan circled lazily overhead, and a light breeze ruffled the leaves of the surrounding palms. Everyone except Aaron ordered a hamburger. It was a French restaurant, and there wasn't a single vegan dish on the menu.

"I'll just have a salad and fries," he told the waiter, lighting one of his special herbal cigarettes.

"We've been having such a wonderful time," gushed Eleanor,

buttering a roll and wolfing it down like she'd been stranded on an island for weeks with no food. She'd gained so much weight since she'd been away, Blair wondered if she ought to say something. "But I'm so glad you kids came."

Cyrus squeezed her arm. "And your mother and I have a great big surprise for you," he said, his blue eyes looking more bulbous than ever.

Eleanor put her diamond-encrusted fingers over his fat lips. "Shh," she said. "Not until Christmas."

Aaron felt Blair's knee touch his beneath the table and instead of pulling away, he left it there. It was one of his twisted little pleasures—the casual knee bump, her hand brushing his as she reached for the bread, her breath on his ear as she sighed with boredom.

He could tell that Blair had just had a shower, even though her hair was dry, because she smelled like her favorite Kiehl's coconut shampoo. He also noticed that her skin was browner than it had been when they were on the plane, so she'd obviously used some kind of tanning lotion just after they'd arrived. He knew her toenails were painted light pink and that she'd taken her watch off. And he hated himself for noticing these things, because these were not things a brother was supposed to notice.

Tyler stared dejectedly into his Coke. He wanted to have his own record label one day and make videos for MTV. Not only did it suck to be only eleven years old and have to spend vacation with his family instead of going to Ozzfest, but everyone else had a friend with them except for him.

"Don't worry, man," Aaron said, noticing his stepbrother's protruding lower lip. "As soon as we're done eating, Miles and I are taking you out jet-skiing."

Tyler fished the straw out of his glass and tried to set it on fire with Aaron's Zippo. "Cool," he said, trying to maintain his eleven-year-old badass image while dressed in absurdly nerdy pleated khaki shorts and a green Lacoste shirt.

Their food came, and Cyrus and Eleanor started to give the highlights of their honeymoon cruise. Last week they'd climbed a volcano and seen stingrays in Martinique. In St. Johns, Cyrus had bought Eleanor a coral-and-diamond pin that had been found in a shipwreck. And on Virgin Gorda they'd had cocktails with Albert Finney, who was supposedly some very famous old actor that none of them had ever heard of.

Serena tuned them out. She and Blair were seated facing the beach, and in the sky above the water a seaplane looped and dived. It soon became apparent that the plane was writing letters in the sky. How did they do that? And wouldn't it be funny if the pilot couldn't spell? She squinted as she read the word drifting in the sky, assuming it would be in French.

S-E-R-E-N-A.

Serena's hand flew to her mouth and she nudged Blair hard with her elbow. Blair nudged Serena back just as hard. She picked up a little folded white card displayed in the center of the table and handed it to Serena.

Serena's fingers were trembling as she read the gold type printed on the card:

Please make your reservations for the Isle de la Paix
Christmas Eve party featuring 45
8 PM–midnight

Serena grabbed Blair's hand and squeezed it tight. The only thing that was going to keep them both sane this Christmas was if they stuck together.

"Oh, look!" Eleanor hissed, causing both Serena and Blair to jump in their seats. She pointed across the restaurant to the reception desk. "It's Misty and Bartholomew Bass!" She lowered her voice to a whisper. "I heard Misty had her liver removed—she has a terrible drinking problem—but she looks all right to me. I wonder if they came down here by boat. What a clever way to dry up. I mean, you can't very well drink on a boat if you don't bring any booze."

Misty and Bartholomew Bass, parents of the infamous Chuck Bass, were checking into the hotel, a pile of Louis Vuitton luggage at their feet. Blair and Serena waited for Chuck to appear beside his parents—it would be just their luck—but there was no sign of him.

"It was her appendix, Mother," said Blair after a moment. It looked like Chuck had stayed home, thank fucking God. "She got appendicitis. No big deal."

"Well, that's not what I heard," Eleanor insisted. "Anyway, I didn't know they were spending Christmas here." She glanced around the restaurant, stroking her coral-and-diamond pin with her fingertips. "I heard there are quite a few celebrity types staying here, too, although I haven't seen anyone I recognize."

Cyrus shut her up by slipping a French fry into her mouth. "Just making sure you're getting all your vitamins and minerals, darling," he said lovingly.

Blair was pretty sure her mother didn't need any extra fries, and she was also pretty sure she didn't want to sit there and watch Cyrus feed them to her. Talk about making her want to puke.

"Excuse me," Blair muttered, and then bolted from the table in search of the nearest ladies' room.

Everyone was so used to Blair jumping up from the table instantaneously that no one thought anything of it, but Serena hated the thought of Blair in a bathroom stall making herself sick. She draped her cloth napkin over her uneaten burger. "Thank you for lunch," she said weakly. Then she got up and hurried after Blair to see if she was okay, keeping her lovely blond head down in case Flow was somewhere nearby, lurking behind a palm tree.

who really wants to know victoria's secret?

"Wait'll you see the stuff I just shot," Vanessa told Dan as she sat down at his father's dining room table. Jenny and Nate weren't there yet, but Rufus had drunk too much red wine and couldn't wait to eat. "It's totally crazy. You're going to be very proud of me."

"So, you're a filmmaker, Vanessamonda?" Dan's father's friend Lyle asked, helping himself to some lasagna. "What sort of films do you make?"

Vanessa took a sip of water. "Black and white. You know. Not much action."

Lyle filled the rest of his plate up with baked beans, the side dish Rufus had chosen to serve with the lasagna. "Artsy movies, eh?"

Vanessa nodded. "I guess."

"I'm kind of an adventure film buff myself. Ever seen *The Mummy*? As far as I'm concerned it's the perfect movie."

But Vanessa wasn't listening. Nate and Jenny had just arrived and were busily undressing in the hallway.

"Sorry, Dad," Jenny said breathlessly, removing her hat. Vanessa recognized the hat instantly. It was red and fuzzy, just like the hat the girl in the park had been wearing. And Nate was wearing a long navy blue overcoat, just like the guy in the park. He had the same preppy look, too, and the same wavy golden brown hair. Vanessa put down her fork.

Oops.

"Dad, this is Nate," Jenny said, leading Nate over to the table. She felt like dancing around the table, kissing everyone there. She hadn't known it was possible to feel this happy—Nate had said he loved her!

Nate shook hands with her father. "Nice to meet you, Mr. Humphrey."

Rufus had his mouth full and he washed it down with wine. "Nate, my boy," he said, "you're the reason my daughter has borrowed over four hundred dollars from me in the last month. It's nice to finally meet you." He pulled the chair next to him away from the table. "Come, have a seat."

Jenny was so elated, she didn't even care if her father embarrassed her. She just hoped he'd be nice to Nate.

"So tell me, Nate," Rufus said, pouring a gallon of wine into Nate's glass. "What are you into?"

Nate smiled. Jennifer's dad seemed cool. "Boats," he answered. "My parents have a house up in Mount Desert, Maine. Me and my dad make boats and sail them up there."

Dan waited for Rufus to begin eating Nate alive, railing about the selfishness of the leisure class and the uselessness of things like sailboats, but Rufus appeared to be fascinated and kept on asking Nate questions.

Normally the hypocrisy of this would have driven Dan nuts, but he was too distracted by what he wanted to tell Vanessa to get upset about the fact that his dad was shooting the shit with a spoiled stoner like Nate. He picked at his lasagna. Give it ten more minutes, and then he was going to ask to be excused so he and Vanessa could "talk" in his room.

All of a sudden, Rufus banged on the table. "Hold on, everyone, pass me your plates. I think this lasagna would taste a hell of a lot better if it was flambéed."

"Dad," Jenny whined. He was going to completely embarrass her. It was unavoidable.

Nate handed Rufus his plate. Rufus lit a match and dropped it on Nate's lasagna. There was so much rum in the sauce, the lasagna burst into flames.

"All right!" Nate exclaimed.

Rufus laughed gleefully and Jenny handed him her plate, a thrilled grin plastered to her face. It looked like they were bonding!

Dan couldn't stand it any longer. He turned and bent his head toward Vanessa. "Can I talk to you for a minute?" He was so nervous, his hands were shaking.

"Okay," Vanessa shot back, suddenly nervous, too. Did she dare go through with it and show him her little costume? Lyle took her plate away and then handed it back to her in flames. "Thanks," she murmured distractedly.

Dan stood up. "Come on."

Vanessa picked up her bag and followed him down the long hall to his bedroom. The Humphreys' apartment was one of those rent-controlled relics that hadn't been renovated since the 1940s. It was big and dusty, with creaking wood floors and paint peeling from the walls, and it smelled like old shoes and moldy book bindings. Dan had once found an unopened pack of cards on a shelf in his dad's office that had been printed in 1955. All the kings looked like Elvis Presley. They were awesome.

"So," Dan began awkwardly as he closed his bedroom door. "I wanted to tell you something."

Vanessa sat on the floor and unlaced her black leather combat boots. If she was going to go through with this, she had to just do it quick before she stopped and thought about it. "Uh-huh," she said. She pulled her black wool kneesocks off and wiggled her bare toes. Two nights ago she'd let her sister, Ruby, paint her toenails chocolate brown. They still looked pretty good. She stood up and unbuttoned her black cardigan.

Dan walked over to his desk and picked up his latest black notebook, thinking that maybe if he showed Vanessa how bad his poetry was, she would understand why he had to have sex. He thumbed through the pages. They were full of the beginnings of poems like, *You are my Frankenstein, my Lichtenstein. You are divine.*

None of them had endings because they were all too terrible to finish. Reading them made him blush with embarrassment.

"I can't seem to write anything good anymore," he said, still rifling through the pages.

Vanessa pulled off her black wool skirt. She yanked her black turtleneck off over her close-shaven head. Then she stood with her hands on her hips, waiting for Dan to turn around.

"And I was thinking, maybe the reason I can't write anything is because . . ." Dan closed the notebook and spun around. "I need to—" He stopped short.

Vanessa was standing next to his bed wearing a black lace push-up bra and a pair of black lace short shorts that were both so flimsy and sheer, Dan could see *everything* through them.

Of course. That was the point.

She grinned and batted her eyelashes. "What do you think?"

Dan stared at her, appalled. It was the last thing he'd ever expected to see. "What are you doing?"

Vanessa walked toward him, trying not to think about what her upper thigh and lower butt region looked like in the very high-cut tangas. She put her hands on Dan's shoulders.

His whole body was trembling. She wasn't sure if that was good or bad.

Dan glanced around the room. "You're not filming this, are you?" he asked suspiciously. Usually Vanessa asked him first if he wanted to be in one of her films, but he could see her trying to get something totally raw on film by not telling him about it first.

She shook her head. "Kiss me," she said.

Dan folded his arms over his chest. He could see what Vanessa was up to now.

So? They were in love. Why didn't he just go for it?

Any other guy definitely would have. But Dan wasn't any other guy. He was Dan, the sensitive romantic. He didn't want his first time cluttered with black lace lingerie. It was too premeditated and clichéd and . . . *wrong*. He wanted it to be pure and spontaneous and . . . *right*.

Dan took a step back and turned his head away. "Sorry," he said.

Vanessa understood that she had pushed him and perhaps that wasn't fair, but she'd just been trying to have a little fun. She had also tried to make herself irresistible to him, but he'd obviously been able to resist just fine. She grabbed her shirt from off the bed and quickly pulled it on over her head, feeling completely humiliated.

Dan lit a cigarette and took a long, hard drag. "Want to show me that stuff you filmed in the park?" he asked.

Um. Maybe not.

Vanessa shook her head, unable to look at him. She pulled on her skirt and buttoned up her cardigan.

Dan put out his cigarette in an empty coffee mug. "I guess we should go back to the table, then."

Vanessa tied her bootlaces and stood up. "I think I should

just go," she said, her voice shaking. She hadn't cried since she was about four years old, but it looked like she was about to now.

Dan nodded, feeling torn between asking her to tell him what was wrong and wanting her to leave so he could try to write again. What would they say to each other if she stayed, anyway?

Weird how a thing like having your girlfriend dress in skimpy lingerie can totally change your relationship.

Vanessa walked over to the door and opened it. "'Bye," she said quietly.

"'Bye," answered Dan as the door closed behind her. He went back to his desk, sat down, and opened his notebook, hoping his confusion over what had just happened would inspire him to write something brilliant. But it didn't, and so he just sat there, chain-smoking.

j's art freaks n out

"May we be excused, Dad?" Jenny asked. "I want to show Nate my room."

Rufus barely glanced at her. *"Mais oui,"* he said in a terrible French accent. *"Bien sûr."*

Jenny rolled her eyes. When her dad drank too much red wine, he attempted to take on the persona of a cool Beat poet, smoking cigarettes and speaking French in a bohemian café.

Like father, like son.

"Come on," she told Nate, leading him down the hall to her room. She opened the door and turned on the light.

Nate hadn't expected to be surprised by Jenny's room. The rest of the apartment was kind of comfortable and crumbling, like a country house that had never been cleaned, and he'd expected her room to be more of the same. But Jenny had always hated her plain, off-white walls, her cracked ceiling, her bare wood floor, and her plain old white sheets, and she was actually quite a good artist. So over the past couple of months she had taken up painting, specifically portrait painting, and her favorite subject was, of course, Nate. There were six portraits of him in all, each one done in the style of a different artist. There was Monet Nate, done impressionist style; Picasso Nate, with his eyes in his feet; Dalí Nate, dripping into in a puddle on the sidewalk; Warhol Nate, with his eyes electric green and his hair in gold paint; Pollock Nate, with paint splattered in the shape of a head; and Chagall Nate, with Nate's head flying through a night sky.

"Do you like them?" Jenny asked hopefully. "I'm trying to copy all different styles. The Pollock one was the hardest."

Nate gazed up at the paintings on the walls with his mouth hanging open. He didn't know which one was the Pollock, nor did he recognize any of the other artists' styles Jenny had used, but he recognized himself times six, and that was enough to give him pause.

"So this is where I spend most of my time," Jenny explained gleefully. Nate had been so charming talking to her father, it had made her fall even more in love with him. Bravely, she stood on tiptoe and put her hands on his shoulders. "I've kind of wanted to kiss you all night," she whispered huskily.

Nate stiffened, but not in the way you'd think.

Yes, normally this sort of advance *would* have given him a major boner, but Nate had just gotten a very clear picture of Jenny spending hours alone in her room painting these good but extremely weird portraits of *him*.

The thing was, he had just told Jenny he loved her. And he'd meant it at the time, sort of. But did she now expect him to, like, deflower her or something?

He kissed her lightly on the mouth. "I'd better go soon," he said gently. "I have to pack for tomorrow and stuff."

Jenny frowned. "Oh, please don't leave." She grinned and looked down at the floor. "I'm still wearing my thong."

Nate had to get out of there before she started taking off her clothes right in front of her art collection. Luckily he didn't have to think of a good reason why he needed to leave *immediately*, because just then his cell phone rang.

He pulled it out of his pants pocket and looked at the number flashing on the screen. It was Jeremy. "Hey, man, where are you?" "We're about to meet up at that bar on Rivington. You know, the one where Charlie got kicked out for doing bong hits on the fire escape?"

"Okay, calm down," Nate instructed, thinking that if he made the call sound urgent, Jenny would let him go.

"Huh?" Jeremy said.

"I'll be right there," Nate said. He hung up and grabbed Jenny's hand. "I'm sorry, Jennifer, but I really do have to go. Jeremy said Charlie and Anthony took some bad E and they're freaking out. I gotta go over there and help them before they do any serious damage."

Jenny nodded, her lower lip trembling. Nate was going away to Maine tomorrow. She wasn't going to see him for days and days. "Okay."

He pulled her into a hug. "I'll be back for New Year's Eve. You be good, okay?"

She squeezed her eyes shut and hugged him tight. "I love you." She couldn't get enough of saying it.

Nate let go and grabbed a stuffed panda from her bed. He tucked it under Jenny's arm. "Pretend he's me," he said, kissing her on the nose. And then he shot out of the room and down the hall, showering Mr. Humphrey with polite thankyous before jumping into a taxi headed straight for the bar on Rivington Street, where he was going to buy his friend Jeremy a very large drink to thank him for inadvertently saving his ass.

Disclaimer: All the real names of places, people, and events have been altered or abbreviated to protect the innocent. Namely, me.

hey people!

Sorry it's been so long, but you know the drill: School's out and so am I—*every night!*

So what's with the link?

Okay, so we've all heard about those people on Eyewitness News who tip off the police because they happened to have been out filming their kid playing in the yard when a drive-by shooting occurs and they have the car's plate numbers down on their digital camera or whatever. Well, I've got something here that's sort of the reverse. I *know* who's on the tape, or, in this case, the *link*—but how did it get all over the Internet?

I'm sure you know by now which link I'm talking about. Click on it and you'll find some very excellent coverage of two people we know and love in the park in the snow, pulling their pants down and rolling around together inside a warm winter coat. **J** does have kind of a cute butt, not that I looked that hard or anything. And even inside his boxers, **N**'s butt does not disappoint. No wonder the link is getting passed around the Internet like the latest bootleg 45 concert CD.

Not to name names, but I'm almost positive **V** did the camera work— it's got her artsy angles and steady hand. But why the hell would she put it up on the Web? It just doesn't make sense. If she did post it, she's never going to live it down, and if she didn't, then who did?? I have to say that this is definitely a first: I'm stumped.

Sightings

This just in from the exclusive **Hotel Isle de la Paix** resort on the island of St. Brats, um, I mean **St. Barts**: *Flow* leaving a pet store in

Gustavia—St. Barts' only real town—carrying a birdcage. Don't ask. **Mrs. E.W.R.** vomiting into the wastebasket in the powder room. Now we know where **B** gets it from. **B** and **S** smuggling another pitcher of rum punch into their villa, where they've been hiding since they arrived yesterday. And **A** playing his guitar alone on the beach. He may be cute, but there's nothing sexy about a moping vegan in a LEGALIZE HEMP T-shirt. And back here in NYC: **K** and **I** crying and hugging on **Park Avenue** as they went their separate ways for Christmas. Hmm, maybe they should exchange commitment rings.

Your e-mail

Dear Gossip Girl,
I have a friend whose older sister is friends with **Flow's** publicist, and she told my friend's sister that **Flow** is in St. Barts trying to go cold turkey with his cocaine addiction.
—Brownie

Hey Brownie,
Well, *I've* heard that St. Barts is kind of a drug haven, so if you're right, he's probably not going to last long.
—GG

Deck the halls

Tonight is Christmas Eve. Last chance to buy everything on your list. Last chance to sneak a look under the tree and make sure you're getting the most presents, and if not, to tape new gift tags on the boxes. Last chance to eat as many Godiva dark chocolate truffles as your little heart desires. Last chance to feel five years old again and leave gingerbread cookies out for Santa. It's also the last chance to be very, very nice to the people who are buying you presents so they'll change their minds and decide to buy you that orange pigskin Hermès Birkin bag after all.

Have a v*err*y m*err*y Xmas!

You know you love me,

gossip girl

s and b let boys be boys

"We can't just stay in here all day," Serena told Blair. It was almost noon on Christmas Eve and she was standing at a window of their villa, looking longingly across the deck at the white sandy beach and the turquoise-colored sea beyond.

"But what about Flow and Miles?" Blair reasoned as she squeezed Tom's of Maine fennel toothpaste onto her Braun electric toothbrush. "I thought we were hiding." She'd thought hiding out in the villa with Serena would give her time to work on her Yale essay, but so far all they'd done was drink tall glasses of rum punch garnished with orange slices, maraschino cherries, and paper umbrellas; play bridge; and paint each other's toenails cotton-candy pink. It was time to break out the iBook.

Serena had other ideas. A whole night and half a morning indoors doing nothing was absolutely her limit.

"We're going to the beach," she announced, pulling on a pair of white Miu Miu short shorts over her white bikini bottoms. "And if anyone wants to talk to us, they're going to have to talk to these." She whipped around and pulled away the little white triangles of her bikini top, flashing Blair.

Blair raised her eyebrows and then went back to brushing

her teeth. She spat into the sink. "You mean, go topless?" she asked, liking the idea already.

Serena nodded, a devilish grin playing on her face. "That's exactly what I mean."

Aaron, Miles, and Tyler were having a windsurfing lesson a few feet offshore when Serena and Blair unfurled their canary-yellow beach towels in the sand, removed their bikini tops, and lay down on their backs with their breasts bared to the heavens.

"Gross," said Tyler, turning his back so he didn't have to look.

Miles dropped his sail and fell into the water. He surfaced and shook his head at Aaron, who was still standing on his board. "I can't believe you get to live with that," he said enviously.

Aaron's sail was waterlogged. He yanked hard on the rope, trying to raise it and block his view of the beach, but no matter how hard he pulled, the sail stayed underwater. Blair probably thought she was being European and sophisticated going topless like that, but in his opinion, it was slutty. Anyone who walked by could take a look, and then later on at dinner they'd see her all dressed and be able to imagine exactly what she looked like naked. Thinking about it made him feel dizzy.

Their Speedo-wearing Rastafarian windsurfing instructor, Prinz, waded into the water with his back to the beach. "Let me give you a hand," he said and dove in, dolphinlike, coming up underneath Aaron's sail and pushing it up out of the water with his head.

Nice trick.

Aaron gathered up the slack until the sail was right where it was supposed to be, perpendicular to the board. He gripped the rubber handhold attached to the sail and leaned back as the sail caught the wind. The board skimmed along the surface of the water, making little slapping sounds as it hit the waves and leaving a nice wake in its path. Aaron felt extremely cool. He was doing it!

People began shouting behind him, and he glanced over his shoulder to look.

Serena and Blair were standing on their towels, tops still off, clapping and cheering him on.

"Go, Aaron, go, Aaron! What a stud!"

Aaron stared at them—he couldn't help it—for a second too long. When he turned around again, his board had run aground on a sandy point sticking out into the cove, and he went flying over backward, landing like an overturned crab on his back in the shallow water.

Ouch.

Miles wanted to talk to Blair, but he wasn't sure if there was some unwritten code about how close you could stand next to a girl sunbathing topless without appearing to be leering at her. He also wasn't sure if Blair cared.

Prinz had swum off to rescue Aaron from the sandbar, so Miles pulled his Windsurfer up on shore and walked across the sand until he was standing about eight feet from Blair's towel. Both she and Serena were still lying on their backs. Oh, man, it was a sight to behold.

"Hey," Miles said nonchalantly.

Blair turned her head and squinted at him. This was going to be fun. She sat up, giving him some full frontal nudity. From the waist up, anyway.

"Hi."

Miles looked down at the sand, blushing despite himself. He looked cute in his orange surf shorts and shell necklace, his spiky blond hair sticking up in all directions. "Um, I was just wondering if you're planning to come to the Christmas Eve party tonight."

Blair glanced down at Serena. "Are we planning to go to the Christmas Eve party tonight?" she whispered.

Serena grinned, holding her hand over her eyes like a visor. "Definitely."

Blair turned back to Miles. "Sure we are," she replied.

Miles nodded, trying to keep his eyes on her face. "Cool. See you later."

Blair smiled and shielded her eyes, watching him trudge back to his Windsurfer and show off his muscles as he pushed it back into the water. This *was* fun. How often did guys give you eight feet of breathing room? She lay back on her towel and rolled over onto her stomach.

It may have been fun, but even using SPF 45, there's only so much sun a girl's bare breasts can take!

After an hour and a half of sunbathing, Serena had browned herself thoroughly on both sides. She was about to tell Blair she'd had enough sun when . . .

"Serena?"

She rolled over and sat up.

Yes, it was Flow. And yes, her top was still off.

He didn't seem to mind. He came right up to the edge of Serena's towel and stood over her. Beside her, Blair lay on her stomach, her head covered with a white T-shirt, pretending to be asleep.

"Finally," Flow breathed, shaking his dark curls away from his long-lashed blue eyes. He was wearing electric-orange surf shorts and nothing else, and his lean, muscular body was tanned to buttery cinnamon-toast perfection. Around his neck a shark tooth hung from a leather string. "Did you miss me?"

Serena shrugged her shoulders and rubbed her bare arms, half concealing her bare boobs to keep Flow from getting too good a look. "Well . . . you sent me so many presents. . . ."

He frowned. "Not that many."

Maybe more of the gifts had been from Kati and Isabel than she'd first thought. It was hard to know with those two.

"Well, whatever," Serena said. "Anyway, have you heard the news? Apparently we're engaged."

Flow grinned. "Yeah, I heard that, too. Don't worry about stuff like that. You'll get used to it."

The thing was, Serena was pretty sure she didn't *want* to get used to it. She'd never been out with a rock star before, and she'd had a good time with Flow that one night, but there were so many other guys out there. Rock climbers, photographers, race car drivers, actors, DJs. In a way, Serena was just like that hummingbird she'd been watching last night as he buzzed ceaselessly from flower to flower. She didn't want to hang out on only one flower, draining it for all it was worth. She wanted to taste as many flowers as possible.

Serena dragged her ponytail over her shoulder and examined her split ends, not saying anything. Flow wasn't used to girls acting so blasé in his presence. When was she going to throw her arms around him and tell him how much she'd missed him and how she never wanted to be without him?

"So, my band is playing at the Christmas Eve party tonight," he said finally. "I was hoping maybe we could hang out after so I could give you your Christmas present."

Serena smiled. Oh God, not another present. "I'll be there."

"Cool." He paused, waiting for her to say something else. But she didn't. "All right. See you tonight."

"See you." Serena lay back down again and poked Blair repeatedly in her bare ribs.

"You're such a hypocrite," Blair murmured, rolling over and pulling the T-shirt away from her face.

Serena cocked her head. "How come?"

"You act like you hate all the stuff he gives you, but I bet you can't wait to see what he's giving you for Christmas."

Serena grinned. Blair was right. She could moan all she wanted to about Flow's steady stream of gifts, but girls do like presents, especially ones from famous, criminally good-looking rock stars.

the link explained

"What camera?" Vanessa's twenty-two-year-old sister, Ruby, mumbled. It was three o'clock on Sunday afternoon, but it looked like Ruby had only gone to bed a couple of hours ago. Her eyes were smudged with last night's black eyeliner and she was still wearing her skintight burgundy leather pants. Ruby slept on a futon in what was supposed to be the living room of their one-bedroom second-floor apartment in Williamsburg, Brooklyn. The apartment was filled with equipment—amps and speakers and guitars and microphones for Ruby's band, SugarDaddy, and cameras and lighting equipment for Vanessa's filmmaking. On the floor was a rug their hippy-dippy artist parents had woven themselves on a loom in their house outside of Burlington, Vermont. The rug was army green and candy-apple red and had a Noah's Ark theme, with animals standing in pairs on a green raft floating on a red sea, but it was so littered with Ruby's clothes and sound equipment, the animals were completely hidden.

"My Sony digital video camera," Vanessa persisted furiously. "I left it on top of the kitchen counter." She'd been planning to review the footage of what she'd shot in the park on Friday to see if any of the icicle stuff was worth saving and deleting the footage of Nate and Jenny, but now she couldn't find the camera anywhere.

Ruby rolled over and put a pillow over her face. "I borrowed it."

Vanessa stared at her. Annoyingly, Ruby still had the pillow over her face. "What do you mean, you borrowed it? Where the fuck is it?"

"I loaned it to some friends over at the Five and Dime. They're using it to make a PSA about skateboarding."

"There was stuff on that!" Vanessa shouted in horror. "Stuff for my new film!"

Ruby pulled the pillow off her face and sat up. "As if you don't have about ten other cameras. I'm sorry," she said sarcastically. "I'm sorry I entered your space without permission. Can I have a hug?"

Vanessa glared at her sister with her hands clenched so tightly, her nails were making welts in her palms. *Now* she knew why she'd received fifteen e-mails this morning accusing her of being a lesbian pornographer–Peeping Tom slut. Ruby's friends had obviously done a hell of a lot more than just borrow the camera; they'd taken what was on it and posted it on the fucking *Internet*.

Dan already thought she was perverted. What would he think of her now?

Christmas Eve afternoon, Dan was surfing the Internet, looking for articles on writer's block and how to cure it. Everything he found was so fruity and stupid. *Go for a walk.* As if he didn't already walk the length of Manhattan on a daily basis, ruminating over his inability to write anything coherent. *Take a hot bath.* He hated baths. All they did was put him to sleep. *Exercise.* No, thank you. His diet of cigarettes and coffee was hardly conducive to exercise. One site discussed the merits of dropping acid. Apparently a prizewinning writer had written his entire novel on an acid trip one night and didn't even remember writing it in the morning. But except for drinking at parties, Dan had kept pretty clean throughout high school, and he wasn't about to start dropping acid now. Another site advised trying an exercise where you write the first word that comes to mind and then extrapolate from there. You might wind up with just a grocery list of words, the site said, but even that was better than nothing. Dan decided to try it. He turned to a fresh page in his notebook and held his pen ready.

He wrote down the word *telephone*, but then his computer bleeped, indicating that he had a new e-mail message. He grabbed his mouse and clicked open his inbox. The message was from Zeke, his only good friend at Riverside.

Check out link below, man. —Z

Dan clicked on the link, thinking it was probably just another stupid basketball trivia link Zeke had found. He turned back to his notebook without waiting to see what came up on screen.

Telephone. Now what? He needed another word.

His father knocked on his open door and poked his head into the room. "Hey, Dan, I'm going out for bagels. Any special requests?"

Dan swiveled around in his chair, about to tell his father to bring him back a very large black coffee, but suddenly his father's face turned gruesome as he stared at Dan's computer screen.

"Jennifer Tallulah Humphrey—is that *you!?*" Rufus roared, storming into the room like a rabid bear. He was wearing a torn white *Onion* T-shirt, and his bushy gray hair stuck out wildly from all sides of his head.

Dan swiveled his chair back around to look at his computer screen. The first thing he recognized was Jenny's red hat. Then he saw what looked like her exposed ass in a white thong. Suddenly a guy with wavy golden brown hair pressed his mouth against her ass. The camera quickly cut to the guy pulling his pants down, and then the image cut to the two of them, wrapped tightly into his coat, doing what looked like the nasty.

Father and son watched in horrified disbelief as the footage repeated itself over and over.

"Jennifer!" Rufus bellowed again, spraying the computer screen with angry spittle.

Jenny appeared in the doorway looking like the picture of innocence in a light blue velour sweat suit with her hair pulled back into a curly puff of a ponytail. "What?" she demanded.

Dan pushed back his chair so she could see the screen from where she was standing.

"What?" Jenny repeated impatiently. She took a step forward, and then her hand flew to her mouth at the sight of her bare butt on screen. It was like watching a horror movie in which she was the star. *How could this have happened?* she wondered in complete mortification.

"It's you and that Nate fellow," Rufus pointed out unnecessarily, his face contorted with rage.

He was a liberal parent. He let Dan smoke in his room and drink whenever he wanted. He'd let Jenny buy her first pair of platform shoes when she was nine. But Jenny was still his baby, and to see her writhing around half naked with a boy on the Internet was more than enough to give him a reality check.

Mute with horror, Jenny stared at the screen as the footage repeated itself. There was her hat, her thong, her butt with Nate's head pressed against it, then the two of them rolling around in the snow inside his coat. It had been such a private, special moment, but now it was out there for the whole world—including her father and brother—to see. She let out a squeaky little gasp and bolted from the room.

Rufus looked at the screen for a moment longer and then glowered at Dan. "Do you know anything about this?" Dan shook his head no. Although he felt somehow responsible. He'd been so distracted by his writer's block and waffling back and forth about having sex with Vanessa that he hadn't protected Jenny from that rich, cradle-robbing bastard, Nate.

"Well, from now on I want you to keep an eye on her," Rufus growled. "I may be lenient, but I can't have her running around like some sort of floozy."

Dan nodded solemnly, and Rufus patted him on the shoulder and headed into Jenny's room, where she was lying facedown on her bed with her head buried in a soft goosedown pillow, surrounded by portraits of her beloved Nate.

"Jennifer." Her father controlled his voice as best he could. "I never thought I'd have to do this, but you've given me no choice. For the rest of vacation you are grounded. No going out. No movies. No allowance. No phone calls. No e-mails. No nothing. And certainly no contact with that Nate character. Dan's going to watch you like a hawk and make sure you don't sneak around, because clearly you can't be trusted."

Jenny sat up. Her face was blotchy and her lower lip quivered. "It's not fair!" she protested. "I don't know who did that! It's not my fault! Nate and I are in love! He took me to the *Nutcracker*. We didn't do anything wrong!"

Rufus waved his hand in the air to quiet her. "You're too young to know anything about anything, especially love," he harrumphed gruffly.

"But Dad, I didn't know anyone was filming us," Jenny pleaded, hugging her panda.

Rufus raised his wild, bushy salt-and-pepper eyebrows and rubbed his stubbly chin. "You think that makes it okay?"

"I don't even care!" Jenny cried, throwing her panda on the floor and bringing on a fresh onslaught of angry tears. "I don't care what you think! We didn't do anything *wrong*."

Rufus crouched down and pulled the unread copy of *Anna Karenina* that he'd given her last summer from her bookshelf. He stood up and tossed it on her bed. "I'll tell you what I think," he bellowed. "I think you need to stay indoors reading more books!"

Jenny glared at the book and kicked it childishly until it slid off the bed and fell onto the hardwood floor. Rufus shook his head in disgust and turned and slammed the door behind him before he really lost it.

Dan listened from his room, still staring at the footage repeating itself on his computer screen. Now that he was over the initial shock of seeing his baby sister starring in a pornographic Web movie, he saw that there was something horrifyingly familiar about the camera work. The unusual angles. The way the camera cut so close, the images were almost abstract, and then panned so far back, Nate and Jenny were just a writhing blob in the pure white snow. It was the work of Vanessa Abrams, Dan was sure of it.

He punched the power button on his computer, disgusted with himself for watching for so long, but even more disgusted with Vanessa and Jenny. How was it that they had both turned out to be such . . . Dan picked up his black notebook and instantly thought of a new word to start his writer's block exercise. He picked up his pen and wrote it down.

Sluts.

n hosts a little reunion

You'd think having a country house as far from the city as Mount Desert Island, Maine, would be kind of lonely, but Mount Desert was full of enormous vacation "cottages" owned by New York's oldest and wealthiest families, and the children had all played together during the summers and on holidays since they were toddlers. For high school, most of them went off to different boarding schools all over the East Coast, so when they saw one another on the island again it was like a reunion. Every Fourth of July a huge gang of them built a bonfire on the beach and set off fireworks they'd smuggled in from Canada. And every Christmas Eve, Nate always hooked up with the same two guys and did bong hits in his rec room.

The rec room had oak paneling, an enormous stone fireplace, and a slate floor that was heated by the copper pipes beneath it. Impressive racks of antlers hung from the walls, taken from the deer and moose that Nate's grandfather had hunted himself. There was an oak bar stocked with aged Scottish whiskeys and rare European brandies, and a wine cellar that you got to by climbing down a ladder through a trapdoor beneath the handwoven Persian rug. An antique mahogany pool table with ornately carved mahogany legs and a red felt top stood in the center of the room.

Nate supplied the bong. He'd had it since he was thirteen, and it was covered in Looney Tunes Band-Aids. The other two boys grinned at it like an old buddy that had been through even more wacky shit than they had.

"Dude," said John Gause, who had brought the pot. "It's good to see you."

John was wearing a tan sheepskin vest, faded boot-cut jeans, and a scuffed pair of tan leather cowboy boots. Not a great look, unless you're the Marlboro Man or a Ralph Lauren model, and he was neither one.

A week before finals John had been expelled from Deerfield for dealing, and he'd just returned from ten days on a dude ranch in Wyoming, where he'd been sent to learn values like honesty, trust, and respect for his fellow man.

Nate packed the bowl and handed it to Ryan O'Brien, who was only fifteen but a worse stoner than John and Nate combined. After getting kicked out of St. Jude's the first week of the school year, Ryan had left for Hanover Academy, the boarding school where Serena used to go. "I think you've grown," Nate said. "Doesn't Ryan look more grown-up to you?" he asked John.

Ryan flicked his lighter over the bowl. He was six foot two and had curly black hair that hung down to his shoulders almost exactly like Flow's, only darker. "Fuck off," he said, hitching up his baggy gray Burton snowboarding pants.

Nate waited for Ryan to take a hit and pass him the bong. The sun was setting and the windows in the rec room were glowing pink. It had snowed hard that winter, and the huge house was nestled in an eight-foot drift. Outside, there were no bleeping car alarms or roaring buses. It was completely still. But if Nate listened hard, he could hear the sound of the ocean crashing against the rocks. He loved that sound. Sometimes at night he just lay on his bed, listening to it.

He took a hit, covering the top of the bong so the smoke wouldn't escape. Then he took another one, rewarding himself for spending two whole hours earlier that day reading through his college applications and filling out the easy parts. He exhaled, passed the bong to John, and closed his eyes. It was good to be away from the city—away from school and everyone talking so incessantly about the future. Up here he could just relax and enjoy himself without worrying about exams or college or answering to anyone.

John finished his hit and put the bong down on the pool table. He picked up the white ball and rolled it around in his hand. "So, Nate," he began. "What's with the porno flick on the Internet?"

Nate blinked slowly at him, like a lizard blinking in the sun. "Huh?"

Ryan lit a Marlboro Light and blew a few smoke rings up at the post-and-beam ceiling. "You know," he prompted. "You and that short girl with the curly brown hair and the huge tits?"

Nate nodded. He knew who Ryan was talking about, but for a split second he couldn't remember her name. "Jennifer," he said, suddenly remembering.

"Yeah, okay. Jennifer," Ryan said. "Didn't you see the link?"

Nate shook his head. "What link?"

John grabbed a pool cue from the rack on the wall and twirled it in his hands like a bayonet. "The link that, like, everybody's talking about, man!" He laughed. "I can't believe you haven't seen it!"

Ryan picked up the little blue cube of pool cue chalk, held it under his nose, and sniffed it, as only a very stoned person would do. "It's like a whole movie of you and that Jennifer chick," he explained. "Like, *fucking* in Central Park."

Nate held the bong in front of his face. He didn't remember fucking Jennifer in the park. He didn't remember fucking Jennifer at all. All he remembered were those crazy portraits of him hanging on the walls of her room. He shook his heavy, stoned head and chuckled to himself. A porno flick on the Internet? That was a good one. These guys were always fucking with him. Shrugging it off, he pressed his mouth into the stem of the bong and flicked on the lighter, taking a nice, long Christmas Eve hit. He was on his way to a very mellow place, one where Jennifer and those crazy portraits were just tiny specks in the hazy distance.

The house intercom crackled. Suddenly Nate's father's New England country-club voice filled the room.

"Your mother and I are pouring cocktails in the great room. Won't you join us?"

You'd think this would have been a buzzkill, but Nate always got a kick out of hanging out with his aristocratic parents when he was high. They made the strongest drinks, and besides, it was Christmas Eve.

Nate handed John the bong and hit the button on the intercom. "Be right up." He let go of the button and nodded at John. "Go ahead. One more hit and then you guys better split."

He and Ryan watched John take his final hit.

"So are you and that Jennifer girl, like, still together?" Ryan asked.

Nate grabbed the eight ball and rolled it across the pool table. He tried to remember the way he'd left things with Jennifer, but all he could remember was the stuffed panda that sat on her bed.

It was funny how he kept managing to forget the "I love you" part.

"Nah," he said. "Not really."

John finished his hit and Nate let him and Ryan out the back door of the rec room and into the snow. Then he locked the door, stashed the bong in an old tin of Triscuits under the bar sink, and headed upstairs to drink gin and tonics and eat fresh Maine oysters with his parents.

b's mom lets fly with her surprise

Blair had showered and put on her new gauzy pink dress from Calypso. Now she sat on the wraparound deck smoking a Merit and waiting for Serena to get ready while she thought about Audrey Hepburn.

As if she wasn't *always* thinking about Audrey Hepburn.

Another thing she loved about Audrey that she wanted to discuss in her college essay was Audrey's versatility. No matter what setting she was plunked into or what sort of costume she had to wear—like the schoolmarmish tweed outfit in the bookshop scene in *Funny Face*, or the crazy hat and lace dress from the Ascot scene in *My Fair Lady*—she seemed perfectly at ease, adapting to her surroundings and at the same time maintaining her cool *Audreyness*.

Blair liked to think that *she* would be able to do that when she went off to college. Since she and Nate were obviously not going to live in an off-campus apartment together in New Haven any longer, she might very well have to live in a dorm with some random roommate. She might have to eat in a dining hall, and she'd definitely have to go to class. But no way was she going to start wearing oversized Yale sweatshirts and carrying a backpack. She was going to maintain her dignity, her sense of style, and her unique *herness*.

Blair puffed on her cigarette, trying to imagine Audrey at Yale, dressed in her black *Breakfast at Tiffany's* gown, with her elbow-length black gloves and diamond-and-pearl choker.

And then it hit her. That was exactly what she would do for her essay: make Audrey a Yale student *in a screenplay!*

Ms. Glos had told her to be creative. Well, you couldn't get much more creative than that! Blair leaped to her feet and slammed open the screen door to the villa, eager to start writing immediately. She could skip the stupid Christmas Eve party. Getting into Yale was *so* much more important.

Serena was standing in front of the mirror tying a sea-green beaded pareo around her waist. She was still wearing her wet white bikini, and there was sand in her hair.

"I thought you were getting changed," Blair said.

Serena frowned. "I didn't feel like it." Everyone expected her to get all dolled up and look pretty for Flow, but really, why should she?

The thing was, Serena was still ten times more gorgeous than any other girl on the island no matter what she was wearing.

"So you're wearing your bathing suit?" Blair asked, confused.

Serena nodded. "Uh-huh."

Blair grabbed her iBook out of her bag and flopped down on her bed. "I think you're in denial."

Serena flopped down next to her. "Maybe." She glanced inquisitively at Blair, who was already typing. "What are you writing?"

"A screenplay." Blair typed in her name and December 24 at the top of the page, and then the tentative title: *Audrey Goes to College.* "I think I'm going to skip the party so I can work on it."

"Talk about denial. Miles is totally pumped to hang out with you tonight, and no way am I going to this thing alone,"

Serena declared. She leaned her head on Blair's shoulder. "Don't you want to have a fun Christmas Eve?"

Blair chewed her bottom lip. "I do, but I want to get into Yale more."

Serena reached out and quickly snapped the laptop closed. "Well, I'm going to make sure you get *everything* you want," she cried, jumping up and pulling Blair to her feet. "Please come?"

Blair sighed. Serena had the remarkable ability to go from sulky to perky with the bat of an eyelash. "Okay," she sighed. "But if I don't get into Yale, it's going to be all your fucking fault."

Miles and Aaron were waiting for the girls in the bar. Aaron had rearranged his dreadlocks so that they lay flat on the sides of his head and stuck straight up on top. He wore a black linen jacket over a gray T-shirt and black linen pants, and if he hadn't been Blair's stepbrother, she might even have thought he looked cute.

Aaron thought Blair looked better than cute. Her tan had deepened, and her dark brown hair was streaked with gold from the sun. Her pink dress was loose, but the gauzy material clung to her body in all the right places. She looked like a goddess, but of course he could never tell her that. Aaron was so afraid he might say something inappropriate, he had become almost robotlike in his dealings with Blair. "We'd better go over and sit down," he said to no one in particular. "Your mom and my dad have some big surprise they want to tell us about. They've been waiting for you for almost an hour."

Blair peered into the crowded dining room, where her mother and Cyrus and Tyler were already seated at a table. "Oh God, I can't wait. Please, can I just have one drink first?" she pleaded.

"As long as you drink it fast," Aaron relented.

As if that would be a problem.

Miles smiled at Blair. "You look really pretty."

Silently Aaron kicked himself. He could have said that!

Miles looked pretty fine himself, dressed in a black Armani dress shirt with white buttons, creamy white cotton pants, and leather sandals—a look that only guys with serious style can pull off. Blair smiled back at him despite herself. She might be glad she'd come to the party after all. "Thanks."

Serena adjusted the knot on her pareo and glanced around for any sign of Flow. Some of the tables in the dining room had been pushed into the corners to make room for a dance floor, and a stage equipped with 45's instruments, amps, and microphones had been set up beside the pool. But the band itself was nowhere to be seen.

"They don't start playing until nine," Aaron said, reading her mind. "I asked the bartender."

Serena didn't respond. That was only twenty minutes from now, and it wasn't like she was desperate for Flow to make an appearance, anyway.

Blair polished off her vodka tonic and handed the empty glass to Aaron. "All right, I'm ready."

The restaurant at the Isle de la Paix was the place to be on Christmas Eve. On the far side of the room, the most famous English supermodel in the world was feeding her toddler fish soup, and beside them the very pregnant star of the TV sitcom *Friends* was holding hands with her hunky Hollywood actor husband. The rest of the dining room was packed with bronzed people in designer resortwear picking at the restaurant's special Christmas Eve dinner of whole snapper roasted with the head and tail intact, purple new potatoes tossed in black caviar, and braised wild leeks.

"Don't worry, dear," Eleanor assured Aaron when they sat down. "We ordered you a special meal."

Cyrus ordered two bottles of Cristal, and the waiter returned with champagne flutes and began filling their glasses.

Blair's mother giggled and glanced at Cyrus. He patted her hand reassuringly, and she cleared her throat.

"All right. I don't think I can bear to keep it a secret for a minute longer." Eleanor took a deep breath and sat up very straight. "Cyrus and I are having a baby."

Blair had been contemplating how to begin the first scene in her screenplay when her mother's disturbing words jarred her brain, forever altering her universe. Her face twitched with a combination of disbelief and disgust as she looked up at her mother.

Excuse me?

"I know forty-seven is a bit old to be pregnant, even in New York, but the doctor assures me I'm perfectly healthy and fit and there's nothing to worry about." She giggled. "Except for me getting as big as a house!"

For a moment, no one responded. Cyrus put his arm around Eleanor and gave her a squeeze.

"Don't all go talking at once," he joked awkwardly, rubbing his fat stomach with his free hand.

Serena didn't want to be rude. "That's just so amazing!" she exclaimed, breaking the silence with as much gusto as she could muster.

She jumped out of her seat and leaned across the table to give Eleanor and Cyrus congratulatory kisses on their cheeks, while also giving the rest of the room a good view of her bare midriff. Blair felt like kicking her. Serena wouldn't have been so chipper if it had been her own mother, that was for damn sure.

"When's it due?" Serena asked, sitting down again.

Eleanor beamed back happily. "June eighteenth."

Blair didn't even try to think of something to say. She felt like she'd just been hit in the head by a flying palm tree, and there was a good chance she would never speak again.

Aaron glanced anxiously at Blair and then raised his champagne glass and smiled at his dad and Eleanor. "Congratulations," he said, hoping Blair would join in.

But of course she didn't, not even when he gently nudged her shin with his foot under the table. Next to Blair, Miles drummed his long fingers on the table and shifted uncomfortably in his seat, wishing he could beam himself back to the bar. He'd been friends with Aaron since ninth grade, but this was all a little too intimate for him.

Eleanor reached across the table and took hold of Blair's rigid fingers. "I hope you'll reconsider taking Cyrus's last name now, sweetheart," she said. "We're going to have quite a nice big family now."

Both Tyler and Eleanor had changed their last names to Rose when Eleanor had married Cyrus, but Blair had refused. *Blair Rose?* No, thank you. It sounded like the name of a perfume made especially for Kmart.

"Of course you don't have to decide right now," Eleanor added.

Blair extracted her hand from her mother's. If she hadn't been wedged between Serena and Miles on the white leather banquette, she would have bolted for the ladies' room to hurl. Instead she picked up her champagne flute and downed its contents in one gulp.

"Where's the baby going to sleep?" Tyler asked. He buttered a piece of baguette and stuffed it into his mouth. "Now that Aaron has the guest room."

Eleanor and Cyrus looked at each other as though they hadn't thought about that before. Eleanor shrugged. "Well,

Blair and Aaron are both going off to college next fall. I'm sure they won't mind sharing the guest room when they're home. And then we can turn Blair's room into a nursery!"

Aaron felt his cheeks heat up. Blair narrowed her eyes at her mother and her stupid blond bob in its prissy headband. So now they were taking over her room to house their ugly devil's spawn?

She was revving up to say something to shut her mother's trap before bolting for the ladies' room to puke her guts out, but then, without any introduction, the four members of 45 quietly walked onstage, picked up their instruments, and began to jam. And the music was *loud*. Fantastically, deafeningly loud.

Miles grabbed Blair's hand. "Want to dance?"

Instead of answering, Blair shot out of her seat and practically yanked the tablecloth off the table, pulling Miles along with her.

The band hadn't won the MTV award for being boring—they rocked. And there was no way Serena was going to sit at the table while they played. She grabbed Aaron's and Tyler's hands and dragged them out of their seats. "Come on, you guys," she cried. "Dance with me!"

As soon as Serena's bare feet hit the dance floor, she closed her eyes and let the music take over her body, throwing her wild blond head back, wagging her hips and stomping her feet with abandon. In her white bikini and skimpy sea green pareo, she looked like a mermaid escaped from the sea. Flow couldn't stop staring at her as he belted out the words to the hit song "Karnage." She was every woman he'd ever sung about. His dream girl.

Blair threw all her angry energy into her dancing, punching the air with her fists, kicking her feet out in front of her, thrashing her head and whipping Miles in the face with her long brown hair in a very un-Audreylike manner. Her pink dress clung to her damp sweaty skin, but she didn't care what she looked like anymore. Not that she looked bad. Miles couldn't keep his eyes off of her.

The third song was a slow one, and the dance floor filled up as some of the older couples joined them. Serena shimmied over to Tyler, grinning down at him as she put his hands on her bare hips. Tyler blushed, but he didn't let go. He knew how lucky he was. Even eleven-year-olds have testosterone.

The song was slow and sexy, and Miles slid his hands low on Blair's waist and pulled her head against his chest. Blair didn't pull back. Instead, she pressed herself up against him, hard. Her mind was so full of rage and despair, she was shaking. She didn't want to think about anything; she just wanted to feel good, and thank fucking God she was with Miles, a guy who, yes, wasn't Nate, but who was pretty fucking hot, and she liked him, or at least right now she did. She pulled her head away from Miles's chest and looked up into his almond brown eyes, letting the champagne and vodka rush to her head. Before she could check herself, she pulled his face toward hers and kissed him long and hard as their bodies rocked back and forth in time to the music.

Aaron stood by the bar, alternately watching Blair and Miles and not watching them as he downed first one shot of tequila and then another. He was thankful that Miles could make Blair feel better even if he couldn't. Then again, they were dancing obscenely close and the song was almost over. It couldn't hurt for him to cut in when the next song started. He lit an herbal cigarette, took two quick drags, and then smashed it out in an ashtray, weaving his way around the middle-aged couples on the outskirts of the dance floor as Flow played the final chords of the song.

But when Aaron reached the spot where Blair and Miles had been standing, they were already wandering away with their arms wrapped around each other, strolling through the hibiscus bushes bordering the pool and down the path toward the villas.

Aaron stood in the middle of the crowded dance floor with his hands in the pockets of his black linen pants, watching them go. He couldn't believe he'd actually thought bringing Miles along to St. Barts was a good idea.

The band quickened the tempo, playing "Kiss, Kiss, Kiss," one of their dance hits with a retro ska beat. Still going like a windup toy, Serena bounced over to Aaron and danced a little circle around him. "Come on, party pooper. Take off those poopy pants and dance!" she cried.

Aaron grinned sheepishly and let her pull him into the writhing throng of sweaty dancers. He needed a distraction, and Serena could be extremely distracting when she wanted to be. He yanked off his jacket and threw it into the air, his dreadlocks bobbing as he bopped and grooved.

Serena's pareo came untied and fell to the floor, but she kept on dancing as the music got louder and the tempo increased, shaking her messy blond hair and throwing her arms up over her head. She liked the way Aaron used his whole body when he danced. So many guys just bobbed their heads and shifted from foot to foot, but Aaron was a natural. He looked adorable tonight, too, in his cool black linen pants, with his dreads sticking up on the top of his head. She danced a little closer to him, breathing him in as she shimmied her hips. Why had she never noticed how cute he was before?

Flow watched them dancing, editing the playlist in his head. It was painful enough seeing the love of his life dance half naked with other guys and the least he could do was make damn sure there were no more slow songs.

Too late. Because some people were already dancing to their own private slow song. In bed.

b decides to lose it once and for all

Maybe it was the heat. Or maybe it was the fact that her life was such a complete mess that she wanted to do something drastic to change it. Whatever the reason, Blair knew she was following Miles back to his villa with a purpose: to have sex.

Actually, *he* was following *her*. She was practically dragging him.

"Wouldn't you rather hang out in your room?" Miles asked on the way. He and Aaron and Tyler had kind of trashed their place.

Blair thought she ought to leave their villa to Serena, just in case she needed a place to escape from Flow. "Serena might need it," she said. "You don't think Aaron will mind, do you?"

"Nah." Miles closed the screen door behind them. "I was starting to think you weren't that into me." He winced when he turned on the light. The floor was littered with the three boys' clothes and CDs. There was even a half-eaten banana sitting on his bedside table that the maids had somehow missed when they turned the beds down and left little chocolate mints on the pillows.

A half-eaten banana? How romantic.

But Blair didn't care. She slipped out of her strappy

Jimmy Choo sandals and pulled her dress off over her head, dropping it onto the floor along with the other boys' clothes. All that was left to take off was the skimpy pink La Perla thong she'd worn under her dress.

"I'm into you," she said in her most sultry voice, falling back on Miles's bed. "Come here."

Miles pulled off his shirt, slipped out of his shoes, and lay down next to her. He reached for the chocolate mint on the pillow, unwrapped the gold foil, and fed it to her.

Blair kept the chocolate intact in her mouth, grabbed Miles's head, and kissed him, forcing the mint between his teeth with her tongue. She was no longer interested in emulating Audrey Hepburn in *Breakfast at Tiffany's*. Audrey was over, yesterday's news. She was all about Debbie now, as in *Debbie Does Dallas*.

She reached for his white canvas belt with one hand, slipping her other hand under the elastic waistband of her thong and yanking it down.

Hello, woman—good-bye, little girl!

After another few songs, Serena, Aaron, and Tyler went back to the table to eat their dinner.

"Isn't this fun?" Eleanor said brightly. She had eaten her entire plate of red snapper, caviar-tossed purple potatoes, and wild leeks, and was already working on a warm chocolate soufflé. It was so nice that the children were enjoying themselves. She didn't even mind that Blair and Aaron's handsome young friend hadn't come back to eat.

Aaron frowned down at his plate of cold wilted spinach and braised leeks.

Tyler ripped his fish head off the body and zoomed it through the air toward Aaron like a torpedo. "Watch out!" he yelled. "Flying fish!"

"Tyler Waldorf Rose!" Eleanor hissed.

Aaron swiped at Tyler's hand and the mutilated fish head fell onto his plate. He winced. "That's okay, I wasn't hungry, anyway."

Serena wasn't sure why Aaron was in such a bad mood, but she wanted to help. "Here," she offered, thinking he must be starving. She picked up one of her purple new potatoes and began to dab at it with her napkin. "Will you eat this if I wipe all the caviar off?"

She was so busy preparing Aaron's potato, she didn't even notice that the band had taken a break and Flow was headed her way.

"Serena?" he called, coming up behind her.

Serena looked up. Flow was wearing a black wifebeater and the shark-tooth necklace, and his neck and shoulders were slick with sweat. His dark curly hair hung down over his eyes, his cheeks glowed like polished bronze, and his blue eyes were sparkling with adrenaline.

Serena handed Aaron his potato, picked up her fork, and put a bite of fish in her mouth. "Hi," she said brightly, with her mouth full.

Flow glanced at Eleanor and Cyrus. "Hello," he said.

"Would you like to sit down, son?" Cyrus offered. "You must be beat. Fantastic job up there. Fantastic."

As if he had one clue about rock and roll.

Flow shook his head. "Thanks, but I have to go back on in a second." He turned to Serena again, his brow furrowed fervently. "Do you like the music?"

She laughed and took another bite of fish. Hadn't he seen her dancing like a crazy person out there? "Yeah, you guys are great. You rock."

Flow looked relieved. "Good. Okay. Well, we're just going

to play a couple more songs and then I was hoping I could buy you a drink or something and maybe give you your Christmas present."

Serena took a sip of water. She was kind of pooped from all that dancing. And besides, it wasn't even Christmas yet. "Actually, I'm really kind of tired. How about I meet you for breakfast? You really shouldn't give me my present until Christmas, anyway."

"Breakfast?" Flow said dubiously. After all, he was a rock star. Most of the time he didn't get up before noon.

"Yeah. Around ten-thirty or so?" Serena chirped. "It'll be fun!"

The bass player played a chord and the drummer banged on his drums a few times, letting Flow know the band was waiting for him. "Okay," he said. He leaned down, closed his curly-lashed blue eyes, and kissed Serena on the lips. "Don't forget."

She smiled sweetly up at him. "I won't."

Suddenly the room buzzed with the sound of gossip.

"Did you see that?"

"I heard she's fooling around with the bass player, too."

"Do you think they're really getting married?"

"I heard they're involved in some big drug-smuggling ring."

A few girls screamed as Flow hopped back on stage and picked up his white Fender guitar. He adjusted his micro-phone with his long, delicate fingers and looked out across the clusters of onlookers at one girl.

"This one is for Serena," he murmured, his eyebrows knit-ted together with emotion. Then he broke into the first few chords of his favorite song, "Dark Knight." Now he under-stood where the lyrics had come from and who they were for.

> *Girl, you're my bright star*
> *I'll follow you wherever you are*
> *Fighting off wolves that bite at your heels*

★   ★   ★

Serena sat back in her seat, watching Flow pour his heart out to her. It was hard not to feel flattered. He was so gorgeous, and when he hit those sexy high notes she couldn't help but smile.

All of a sudden Aaron stood up from the table.

"Want to dance?" Serena asked him hopefully.

He shook his head. "I think I'm going to head back to my room," he mumbled.

Serena stood up. Aaron was acting so weird, she was worried about him. "I'll come with you," she offered, forgetting about Flow completely.

Serena followed Aaron around the outside of the dance floor and through the crowd huddled around the bar. Before they started down the path to the villas, she caught a glimpse of the still, green sea and the perfect white beach glowing in the moonlight and was reminded of those summer nights up at Blair's dad's beach house in Newport when she and Blair used to drink martinis and then tear out of the house and across the sand and skinny-dip in the cold, clear water.

Serena couldn't resist. "Let's go swimming!"

Aaron stayed where he was. "Nah," he said. "You go ahead."

"You sure?"

He nodded. "But don't go out too far."

"Okay!" Serena called, breaking into a run. She dashed across the beach, splashed into the waves, and dove in, eager to feel the head-to-toe rush when the cool water enveloped her. Swimming seal-like, she stayed underwater until her head finally broke the surface and she sucked in an exalted breath of night air. Sometimes it just felt good to be alive.

it sucks when you can't find your clothes

Blair just wanted to get it over with quickly, but Miles wanted to take his time, going over every inch of her body in a way that seemed almost clinical, like he was a dermatologist checking her skin for eczema or melanoma or something. She tried to relax and enjoy the feeling of Miles licking her instep, but they were both completely naked and she couldn't help thinking that if Miles had been Nate, they would have done it by now.

When Nate got horny he got sort of violent. Not in a scary way, but in a kind of trembling, unstoppable, passionate way. Blair had always had to be very firm when she said no, she wasn't ready to go all the way, and then she'd had to find a way to distract him.

Oh? Like how?

This time she wouldn't have told Nate to stop, and by now they would be lying in each other's arms, looking at the stars through the window, smoking cigarettes, and talking lazily about the future.

Miles started on the other foot, biting the tip of her big toe and working his tongue over the prickly surface of her diamond toe ring. Blair flinched involuntarily. Everything always seemed so right when she was with Nate. They were like the corner pieces of a jigsaw puzzle. They fit together perfectly, and when they were together, everything else made sense. Which was why it no longer made any sense that she was lying butt naked in a bed in a hotel room on an island in the middle of the Caribbean while a naked Miles licked her feet, and Nate was up in freezing cold Maine all alone, possibly, hopefully, thinking about her.

Blair yanked her big toe out of Miles's mouth and rolled off the bed.

Miles ducked his head out from under the sheet. "What's wrong?"

"I have to go," she said without even looking at him. She crouched down, hunting for her dress, but it was dark and there was so much crap on the floor, she couldn't find it.

Miles slouched on the end of the bed, watching her as he drummed his fingers against his legs. "I was trying to take it slow."

We *know*.

Blair ignored him. "Where's my fucking dress?" she muttered.

Suddenly the lights came on and her dress became extremely visible in a heap on the floor at the foot of the bed. Aaron stood in the doorway, but instead of apologizing quickly and ducking out of the room the way a stepbrother should have, he stared at Blair and continued to stare.

At first Blair was completely embarrassed. Within two seconds her embarrassment turned to anger. *How dare he?* How dare he stare at her like that? He was her freaking stepbrother.

Aaron knew he should turn around and leave them alone, but his feet wouldn't move. Miles bent down and snatched Blair's pink dress up from where it was lying on the floor at his feet. "Dude," he said to Aaron, tossing the dress to her.

Blair pulled the dress on over her head and marched

toward the door. "What's *your* problem?" she hissed, brushing past Aaron on her way out.

Not that she really wanted to know. The villa Blair and Serena shared was only twenty feet away—not far enough, as far as Blair was concerned. She kept on walking past the villas to the beach, and as soon as her feet hit the sand, she started to run. She didn't care that she'd special-ordered the pink dress from Calypso and paid an extra hundred and fifty dollars for it. She ran as fast as she could until she hit the water and threw herself into the waves, ruining the dress for sure. Taking a giant gulp of air, she plunged underwater, hurtling her body forward with all the strength in her arms and legs. Then, when her lungs were about to burst, she came up, gasping and blinking the salt water from her eyes.

The moon was bright and music from the Christmas Eve party echoed from off the water. 45 had stopped and a DJ was playing "Blame It on the Boogie," a vintage Michael Jackson song. On the beach Blair could see the vague silhouette of a girl, her feet splashing in the shallow water, looking like Halle Berry in *Die Another Day*, but with long blond hair and wearing a white bikini instead of an orange one.

Of course it was Serena.

"Where's Miles?" Serena called, cupping her hands over her mouth.

"Who cares?" Blair called back, treading water. "Where's Flow?"

"Who cares?" Serena shouted back.

They both laughed, and Blair floated on her back for a few seconds, looking up at the moon. Then she turned over and swam toward Serena. "I'm thinking of going back tomorrow," she said, getting out of the water. She had a screenplay to write, and she wanted to work on it without her pregnant mother, her weirdo stepbrother, or his stalking friend around to bother her.

Serena knew better than to ask what had happened. "But tomorrow is Christmas," she pointed out. "Won't your mom be pissed?"

Blair squeezed the water out of her hair and it dripped on the sand, leaving a trail behind her. "As if I care. Besides, Cyrus is Jewish."

The two girls walked slowly down the beach and back to their villa, relishing each other's company and the soothing sounds of the waves breaking on shore. If only they could have carried on walking forever.

When they finally reached the villa, they found what looked like a large wrought-iron birdcage covered with a red-and-white gingham dustcover waiting for them by the door.

Merry Christmas!

Serena picked up the birdcage by its brass handle and carried it inside. She put the cage down on top of her bed-side table and pulled off the dustcover as Blair flicked on the light.

Inside the cage a gorgeous green-and-blue parrot with a yellow beak perched on a tiny wooden swing. The parrot blinked up at Serena with its beady eyes. "I love you, Serena! I love you, Serena!" it squawked. "Marry me. Marry me."

Blair snorted. "Do you think it's from Kati and Isabel?"

Serena giggled back. "I don't know. There's no card."

"I love you, Serena! Marry me. Marry me," the parrot said again and ruffled its feathers.

Serena slid the dustcover back on and stepped away from the cage. Flow might have been insanely gorgeous and flatteringly generous, but this was going *way* too far. She looked up at Blair. "You know what you said about leaving tomorrow?"

"Yeah?" Blair peeled off her soaking wet dress and threw it in the direction of the wastebasket in the corner.

Serena walked over to the closet and pulled her red Kate Spade suitcase down from the top shelf. "I'm ready when you are."

topics ◀ **previous**   **next** ▶   **post a question**   **reply**

Disclaimer: All the real names of places, people, and events have been altered or abbreviated to protect the innocent. Namely, me.

hey people!

Ho, ho, ho and Merry Christmas to all!

I know **V**'s family doesn't do Christmas, but I have a present for her, anyway. It seems that something good may come of that link that's been floating around the Internet after all. See below:

Dear Gossip Girl,
My name is **Ken Mogul** and I'm an independent filmmaker. You may have seen my movie *Seahorse*, starring **Chloë Sevigny** and **Tobey Maguire**, which is now out on DVD. I happened to see the footage on the link that you discussed on your site, and I wanted to ask if you knew how to get in touch with the person who shot it. Whoever it is is very talented, and I would very much like to work with him or her. Thanks a lot, and by the way, you rock.
—xoKM

I took the liberty of playing Santa Claus and fairy godmother all wrapped into one and gave **Mr. Mogul V**'s name and told him that she lived in Brooklyn. Look out, **V**: today Internet pornos, tomorrow the Cannes Film Festival!

The rest of your e-mail

 Hi gg,
had to tell you I heard **S** has gone back to her druggy ways. the whole rumor that she and **Flow** are engaged is totally bogus. the real reason she even went to st. barts was to find a dealer so she can bring back a whole load of stuff to sell. Thought everyone should know.
—insider

Hey insider,
You may be right. I heard she's thinking of throwing her own New Year's bash, too. But don't forget, she still has to make it through airport security.
—GG

Dear Gossip Gurl,
i have a house up in Mt. Desert Maine and i met up with some friends there to go tobogganing including **N**. i thought he had a girlfriend but he was flirting with all the girls there including me and he was so stoned i didn't want to ride with him steering the toboggan. L
—pumpkin

Dear pumpkin,
Sounds like **N** is just doing some soul-searching. He can steer my toboggan anytime. J
—GG

Sightings

B and **S** catching a taxi from **JFK** to **Fifth Avenue**, looking gorgeously tanned and happy to be home. **K** and **I** reunited again, in **Williams Sonoma** on Madison, checking to see if **S** and **Flow** have registered for wedding gifts yet. A buff guy in an **Isle de la Paix** staff T-shirt returning a large green-and-blue parrot to a pet shop in **Gustavia**.

One final wish

So, I got just about everything on my Christmas list, even the orange pigskin Hermès Birkin bag. I know you think I'm spoiled, but I deserve it. What I still haven't gotten because it's still six days away is a life-changing New Year's Eve. Let's hope **S** *does* have a party, and who knows—**Flow** might even turn up!

See you there at midnight!

You know you love me,

gossip girl

locked in a tower

Stuck in the house with nothing to do but read and day-dream, Jenny felt like Rapunzel, only with shorter hair and bigger boobs. She put her white satin thong away in the back of her underwear drawer until the next time she'd see Nate. New Year's Eve wasn't too far away, and maybe she wouldn't even have to wait that long. She was secretly hoping he'd miss her so much, he'd come back from Maine and sneak up to her room in the middle of the night via the fire escape. Imagining what they'd do when they saw each other again kept her occupied for hours.

Poor Nate, trapped up there in cold, snowy Maine. Yesterday was Christmas, and he'd probably spent the whole day watching old movies with his parents, every now and then looking out at the snow and wondering when he was going to hear her voice again. Jenny didn't even mind not talking to him on the phone—this forced separation was only making their love that much stronger—but she still had to do something to show Nate that she was thinking of him and loved him more than ever before. Which was why she'd decided to send him a care package.

First she found an old Nike shoe box, which she lined with tinfoil. Then she put a well-worn paperback copy of

Shakespeare's *Romeo and Juliet* into the box. The plight of the lovers in the tragic play was so much like their own: They were deeply in love and had been forbidden to see each other, yet love would win out in the end. Of course, she and Nate wouldn't die, the way Romeo and Juliet had. They'd get married and have a big family and tell stories to their grandchildren about how they'd met in the park one sunny autumn day when all the forces in the universe were perfectly aligned.

Next, Jenny added a foil package of two blueberry Pop-Tarts to the box. They were one of her favorite foods, although she rarely ate them because they had too many calories and absolutely no nutritional value. But she liked the idea of Nate eating something she loved to eat and missing her.

Then Jenny added a picture of her that Dan had taken last summer. She was wearing a yellow tank dress and standing at the edge of a swimming pool at a motel in Hershey, Pennsylvania, where Rufus had taken them to get away from the city one weekend. She liked how shiny her hair looked in the picture, and how her tan arms covered the sides of her boobs so you couldn't tell how big they were.

Next, she put in the playbill she'd saved from the *Nutcracker*. Jenny wanted Nate to know that, starting with the *Nutcracker*, that day had been the most amazing day in her life, the day they had said, "I love you."

Finally, she cut off a thick lock of her curly brown hair, tied it with red thread, and dropped it inside the box. It looked a little strange with all the other things, like a memento of a dead person or something, but she wanted Nate to feel like she was right there with him, and that seemed to be the best way.

With the addition of the lock of hair, the care package felt complete, so she closed the box and taped the lid shut. Then she wrapped it with pages from various teen magazines she had lying around in her room, being careful not to include any pages with embarrassing ads for tampons, birth control pills, or yeast infection medications. Finally, she taped a yellow Post-it to it and carefully wrote out Nate's address in Maine, which she'd written down in her address book along with the addresses of all his family's other houses in Montauk, Nice, St. Anton, and Barbados, just in case.

After sticking the box with twenty stamps she'd stolen from her father's desk drawer, Jenny carried the parcel into the kitchen and opened the back door to leave it for the postman. That was the great thing about living in an old building like hers. There were no mailboxes downstairs, so the postman rode the service elevator and delivered mail right to their back door. She placed the box on the floor beneath the little rack where the postman put the mail and frowned down at it, wondering if maybe she ought to open it up again and put her thong inside to make the care package a little sexier. On second thought, that seemed sort of slutty. Besides, Nate had given her the thong for Christmas. He might think she didn't like it if she sent it back to him.

Dan came into the kitchen and saw Jenny standing in the back doorway. "What are you doing?" he asked suspiciously. Their dad had asked Dan to keep an eye on Jenny, and he was taking his job very seriously.

Jenny closed the back door. "Just seeing if there's any mail." She turned and squinted at Dan. His hair was matted, and he'd been wearing the same coffee-stained white T-shirt for two days. "You look awful."

Dan spooned instant coffee into his cup and ran the hot water tap until it was hot enough to dissolve the crystals. He filled the cup and took a sip. "I'm working on a poem," he said, as if that explained everything.

Jenny opened the refrigerator, reached for a container of Dannon coffee yogurt, and then withdrew her hand and slammed the door closed again. The last thing she wanted was to get fat before she saw Nate again.

Dan blew into his cup, watching her. "You know it was Vanessa, right?" he said stonily. "Who filmed you guys in the park?"

Jenny turned around, tugging down her bra where it had ridden up between her boobs. She hadn't returned to the site since she'd seen it on Dan's computer, and it had never occurred to her to try and figure out who had done it. The idea of Vanessa posting the site seemed absolutely ludicrous.

"How do you know?" Jenny demanded.

Dan shrugged. "Watch the film. It had to have been Vanessa."

Jenny crossed her arms over her chest. "I'd rather not," she said. "Anyway, so what if it was her?" Jenny worked with Vanessa on *Rancor*, the Constance Billard student-run arts magazine, and they had always gotten along fine. If Vanessa had filmed Nate and Jenny in the park, she probably had a perfectly good explanation for why she'd done it and a perfectly good explanation for how it had wound up on the Web.

"I just thought you'd want to know, that's all," Dan said and went back to his room. He'd been arranging and rearranging the list of words he'd written down for that writer's-block exercise, and now he was trying to assemble them in some kind of order for his poem, "Sluts."

Whore, slave, shaved, black, lace, ice, cold, rain, weep, wipe, sleep, coffee, stain, blame . . .

It was going to be an angry poem, of course, but it wasn't *about* being angry. It was about finding out that the person you love isn't the person you thought they were. Jenny wasn't the sweet, innocent little sister he'd thought she was, and

Vanessa was a slutty-underwear-wearing Peeping Tom who used other people's private moments to get attention.

He started pulling words from his list, adding the occasional verb or adjective for embellishment.

Wipe the sleep from my eyes and pour me another cup.
I see what you've been trying to tell me all along,
Shaving your head and handling me (so delicately)
With satin and lace:
You're a whore.

Dan liked the directness of what he'd written, and its energy. He kept writing, invigorated by the feeling of filling up a page again. Once he was finished, he was going to e-mail it to Vanessa. Writing the poem was the only way he knew how to figure out how he felt, and sending her the poem was the only way he knew how to tell her.

v finds a way to apologize

Ruby popped her head into Vanessa's room. She was wearing a black rubber jacket, jeans, and pointy black shoes with spiky heels. She'd cut her black bangs with a razor blade and they were supershort.

"Any mail?" Ruby asked.

Vanessa shook her head. Their parents were traveling around Europe, touring with some art fair, and they had yet to send even a postcard.

"Phone calls? Messages?"

Vanessa shook her head again.

"Any chance you want to come out with me?" Ruby offered. "You're supposed to be on vacation, you know."

Vanessa shrugged her shoulders and zipped her black hooded sweatshirt up to her chin. She was still mad at her sister for taking her camera without asking, and she didn't feel like doing anything except maybe talking to Dan.

Vanessa hadn't talked to Dan since she'd left his house on Friday—the longest stretch of time they'd gone without talking since they'd become friends three years ago. She wanted to explain everything to him, how the whole Web link debacle was just a terrible accident, and how she'd only bought the

Victoria's Secret underwear because she thought it would help him relax and have fun. She wanted to tell him that they had been friends for too long to stay mad at each other like this and to apologize in a million different ways. But she was secretly hoping Dan knew her well enough to guess that she would never have posted a site exploiting his sister like that. And she was secretly hoping that he'd realize he'd humiliated her as she stood there practically naked in her skimpy underwear, and that he'd be the one to apologize first.

"All right. See you later. I'll bring you back some takeout," Ruby said, turning to go.

Vanessa walked over to her computer to check for the hundredth time to see whether Dan had sent an e-mail.

This time, he had! And it was a poem! She pulled up her desk chair eagerly and double-clicked on the file. As soon as it opened, she began to read.

She read the poem three times on-screen before printing it out and reading it again. The words were ugly and angry and they broke her heart. Dan hadn't forgiven her, that much was clear.

But Vanessa had always been able to see the beauty in ugly things, and she'd read enough submissions to *Rancor* to know that this poem was special. It was filled with rich metaphors and passionate language, and while it made her want to bury her head in the covers and sob, she couldn't help but admire the clever turns of phrase. It was brilliant.

Even if Dan never spoke to her again, and even though the poem was all about her and what a horrible person he thought she was, she was going to get the poem published.

Dan had never even tried to publish anything, but there

was no way he wouldn't be astounded when he opened up a copy of *The New Yorker* and saw his poem "Sluts" printed inside. And what an amazing way to impress the colleges he was applying to. She couldn't not do it. She owed it to him.

Jumping up from her chair, Vanessa prowled around Ruby's room until she found a copy of *The New Yorker* wedged under the closet door. She thumbed through it until she found the name of the submissions editor and then went back to the computer and wrote the editor a letter, putting Dan's name and address on the self-addressed stamped return envelope.

audrey goes to college

EXT. ENGLISH DEPT. BUILDING ON NEW ENGLAND COLLEGE
CAMPUS–DAY

A four-story brick building with white columns and
ivy. Green lawn in front. Marble steps.

Eighteen-year-old AUDREY, a beautiful dark-haired
girl in a fashionable skirt and blouse and flat
shoes, rides her classic Schwinn bike across the
lawn and parks it on a rack to one side of the marble
steps. She runs up the steps and goes inside.

INT. ENGLISH DEPT. BUILDING—CONTINUOUS

A long hallway flanked by small department offices.
All the office doors are open, and inside each one
of them a professor is meeting with a student and
discussing the finer points of literature.

                    STUDENT A
          I really thought it would have been better

if the whale could talk, sir.

PROFESSOR A
But it's not about a talking whale. It's about man's search for meaning.

STUDENT B
There's no punctuation. See? I didn't use a single comma or period.

PROFESSOR B
That doesn't make it a poem. A poem has . . . well, a poem has *poetry* in it.

PROFESSOR C
Did you read the book I told you about?

STUDENT C
The one about the whale?

PROFESSOR C
Uh-huh. What'd you think?

STUDENT C
Well, I really thought it would have been better if the whale could talk.

A fourth professor steps outside his door, glances down the hall in both directions, and then slams his door. AUDREY runs down the hall, looking frazzled. She knocks on the door the professor has just slammed shut.

                         AUDREY
          Professor Weeks! Oh, Professor Weeks!

He opens the door.

                         PROF. WEEKS
               You're late.

                         AUDREY
          Yes, but I have a perfectly good excuse.

The professor pauses, waiting to hear her excuse.

                         PROF. WEEKS
               Yes?

                         AUDREY
                    (Breathlessly)
          Oh, but I can't tell you! It's something
          illegal.

                         PROF. WEEKS
                    (Frowning)
          Illegal? Do I need to call campus security?

                         AUDREY
                    (Shaking her head)
          Oh, no. At least, not yet.

She hands him her paper.

                              AUDREY
          I couldn't make up my mind which
          Shakespeare play to write it on, so I wrote
          about all of them. I hope you don't mind.

The professor puts on his reading glasses and
begins to read her paper. He sits down at his
desk, thoroughly absorbed in what he's reading.
As he continues to read, Audrey casually walks
out of his office and closes the door behind her.
She walks down the hall and out the door of the
building, gets back on her bike, and rides away
across the lawn.

EXT. COLLEGE QUAD—CONTINUOUS

A huge lawn triangulated by brick buildings.

AUDREY rides across the lawn, looking up at the
fall foliage instead of looking where she is going.
She crashes into a boy in a crew team sweatshirt on
his way to practice. The boy falls to the ground.

He is COLIN DAVIS

                              COLIN
          Ow!

Audrey gets off her bike and crouches at his side.

                              AUDREY
          I'm so sorry. Are you all right?

                    COLIN
          I think my leg might be broken.

He tries to move it.

                    COLIN
          Ow!

                    AUDREY
          Don't move. I'm calling an ambulance.

She fumbles in her purse for her cell phone. A
gun falls out of the purse and onto the ground.
COLIN stares at it. AUDREY picks up the gun and
shoves it back into her bag. She clicks open her
cell phone and dials 911.

s gets all the balls rolling

Serena had decided that the only way to make up for their lame Christmas was to have a truly awesome New Year's Eve, and the best way to insure that she did was to host her own party. She adored planning parties and was extremely good at it, but it was already Wednesday and there were only three and a half days left to get organized. Blair was no help. She was holed up in her room with her iBook, a carton of cigarettes, and an espresso machine, and she wasn't coming out until she had finished the screenplay she was writing for her Yale application. Serena had always been better at delegating authority than doing all the work herself, so who better to call upon than the two girls who wanted so desperately to be her new best friends?

"Hello? Kati? It's Serena."

"Hi!"

"Listen, is Isabel there?"

"Uh-huh."

Of course she was.

"Cool. So, I was wondering if you guys would mind coming over and helping me plan my New Year's Eve party? I kind of decided to have one at the last minute and I really want it to be good, but I'm running out of time."

The two girls were speechless. Then they both began to squeal.

"Oh my God! It's going to be the best party *ever!* Don't worry, we'll come *right over.*"

And they did.

Serena came to the door wearing red velvet Juicy Couture sweatpants and a tiny little T-shirt with a picture of a snowman on it.

"Oh my God, you're so *tan*," Isabel crowed, kissing her on the cheek.

"Did you lose weight?" Kati added, kissing her, too.

As if Serena needed to lose weight.

Ever the gracious hostess, Serena led them into the living room of her family's enormous Fifth Avenue apartment overlooking the Metropolitan Museum of Art. Her parents were up in Ridgefield for the holidays and her brother was in Boston with his college friends, so she had the place to herself.

She had already laid out several sheets of white paper on the enormous glass coffee table and written headings on them: *Venue. Booze/Food. Music/Sound. Theme/Decorations/Lighting. Invitations. Guest List.* She handed the sheets of paper to Kati and Isabel.

See how good she is at delegating?

"You guys were on the organizing committee for the *Kiss on the Lips* party in October, right?"

They nodded.

"Great. Can you call the same caterer and room designer who did that party?"

"Sure!" Isabel lunged into her bag for her PalmPilot.

"And we'll need to find a cool DJ," Serena instructed.

Kati looked confused. "Isn't 45 going to play?"

Serena blinked. She had no idea what Flow's New Year's Eve plans were, but she was pretty sure she didn't want him chasing her around her own party. "No, actually, they're busy recording their new album," she fibbed. "A DJ's better, anyway. More variety."

The two girls looked disappointed.

"I thought we could just use this old guest list from the Black-and-White Ball," Serena continued, picking up another set of pages from the coffee table. "Of course, you guys can add whoever you want."

Isabel peered at the list. "Is Flow coming, at least?"

Serena faltered. If she said he wasn't coming, then Kati and Isabel would probably start the rumor mill going again, about how Serena and Flow's engagement was off and blah, blah, blah. And it might be a nice gesture to send an invitation to Flow's house in Malibu, especially after she'd left his parrot at the front desk at the resort in St. Barts and flown back to New York on Christmas morning, completely standing him up. It wasn't like he'd actually come to the party, anyway.

"He promised me he would," she said, pointing to Flow's name on the list.

Without thinking about what she was doing, Serena thumbed through the guest list until she reached the Rs, checking to make sure that Aaron Rose's name was there. Aaron wouldn't be back from St. Barts until the thirtieth, but she hoped he'd come to the party. He looked so sad the last time she saw him, she wanted to do something to cheer him up.

"Do you want me to take care of the invitations?" Kati asked, all business. She whipped her Nokia phone out of her red Hervé Chapelier tote bag. "I can call the stationer right now."

"Good," Serena said. "And Isabel, why don't you call the party location service? Tell them we want a big loft downtown with a good view of the fireworks. Preferably with a deck."

As she handed the guest list over to Kati, a name at the

top of the list caught Serena's eye: Nathaniel Archibald. *Where the hell was Nate these days, anyway?* she wondered. He had to come to her party. New Year's Eve just wouldn't be the same without him there.

Nate was busy opening Jenny's care package, which was no simple task, since it was wrapped in a two-inch layer of teen magazines and Scotch tape. The package had arrived yesterday afternoon, but somehow between snowboarding down Cadillac Mountain with John and Ryan and smoking hash in some girl's hot tub at a party in Bar Harbor, he just hadn't gotten around to opening it.

The only clean pair of boxers Nate had left in his drawer were the ones Jenny had bought him at Barneys, so he was now sitting on the floor wearing the sailboat boxers and ripping through the teen magazine pages covering the shoe box the care package had come in, just exactly the way Jenny had imagined it.

He lifted the lid off the box and looked inside, chuckling to himself as he fingered the lock of Jenny's hair. Sending a lock of hair almost seemed like something Blair would do, except she would probably douse it with perfume first and then put it in a silver box from Tiffany lined with red velvet and monogrammed with Nate's initials or something. Nate pulled out the playbill from the *Nutcracker* and thumbed through it. Instead of thinking back to five days ago, when he'd taken Jenny to see the ballet and they'd sat in the first row of the balcony at the New York State Theater in Lincoln Center holding hands as the nutcracker's army of toy soldiers fought off the evil mice under that wicked-big Christmas tree, he thought back instead to the last time he had taken Blair to the same ballet.

Blair had had cramps, so at intermission Nate had gotten

some Advil and a Perrier for her from the bartender, and then they'd gone outside to smoke cigarettes on the balcony. They wound up kissing and spent the whole second act out there, smoking and kissing and watching people walk past the empty fountain and through Lincoln Center. Blair had been wearing a camel-hair coat with a mink collar that Nate liked to press his face into, breathing in the combined scents of animal fur, Blair's perfume, and cigarette smoke.

From on top of the maple Shaker chest of drawers in Nate's Mount Desert bedroom, his cell phone rang. The phone had nine voicemail messages on it, all from Jenny's home number, and Nate hadn't yet dealt with answering any of them. But this time the number flashing on the screen was different.

Nate grinned. He was always happy to hear from Serena.

Yeah, so is every other guy on the planet.

"Hey. What's up?"

"Natie?" Serena's voice chimed over the airwaves. "I just wondered when we're ever going to see you again," she said. "Or are you gonna, like, stay up in Maine until graduation?"

Nate bent down and grabbed the foil packet of blueberry Pop-Tarts out of Jenny's care package. He ripped it open with his teeth and pulled out one of the Pop-Tarts, wolfing it down before he tossed the packet back in the shoe box. "I think I'm going to hang out here for a while longer." He wanted to put off dealing with Jennifer until the very last minute. Or forever, if possible.

"But I'm having a New Year's Eve party," Serena said in a pouty voice. "Kati and Isabel are here right now, helping me plan. We're going to have a kick-ass theme and the best DJ and a huge deck so we can all watch the fireworks. You're a loser if you don't come, and I absolutely promise you'll regret it."

Nate chuckled. The party did sound cool. Then he thought of something.

"Hey, where's Blair? Aren't you guys still in St. Barts?"

"We came home early." Serena sighed. "Blair's being a nerd and working on her Yale application."

"Oh." Nate picked up the copy of *Romeo and Juliet* and ran his thumb across the edges of the dog-eared pages. Then he looked at the cover—a classic painting of a boy and a girl entwined in an embrace. "She's coming to the party, though, right?"

"Of course, silly," Serena exclaimed. "She's not *that* nerdy."

"All right," Nate agreed, still holding the book. "I'll be there."

Serena clicked off. Across from her, seated on the red-and-white chintz love seat, Kati and Isabel were talking busily on their cell phones, booking the caterer and ordering more booze than they would ever need. Serena smiled to herself. It was kind of interesting how Nate had only said he'd come to the party *after* she'd mentioned that Blair was going to be there. She had a feeling it was going to be a very interesting New Year's Eve indeed.

tormented artistes break into the big time

Still wearing the same coffee-stained white T-shirt he'd been wearing for almost a week, Dan had almost filled up a whole new black notebook full of morbid poems about how love was just a pathetic hoax made up by Hallmark to sell Valentine's Day cards and give people the false impression that their lives had meaning. Right now he was working on one called "Car Full of Rocks," about a guy who fills up his car with rocks and drives it into a river because the car reminds him of his ex-girlfriend who liked to drive around and listen to static on the car radio instead of music.

Jenny knocked on his door. "There's mail for you, Mr. Hermit Man."

Dan put down his pen and opened the door. Jenny was wearing her pink bathrobe and had a mustache of white goopy cream above her lip. She handed him an envelope.

"What's that on your face?" he asked, taking the letter.

"I'm depilating," she said, turning away and heading down the hall toward the bathroom.

Whatever the hell that means, Dan thought, closing the door. Clearly Jenny had been spending way too much time trapped in the house reading fashion magazines, but it served her right for being such a slut.

Dan turned the thin white envelope over and examined the return address. It was from *The New Yorker*, probably a letter asking him to subscribe, when his dad was already a lifetime subscriber. He tore it open and unfolded the two pieces of white paper that were tucked inside.

> Dear Mr. Humphrey,
> Thank you for submitting your poem, "Sluts," to *The New Yorker*. Congratulations! I am very pleased to inform you that we will be publishing the poem in our Valentine's Day issue. If you would please fill out the Writer's Information form attached here, we can include some information about you on our Contributors page. A check for eight hundred dollars will follow.
> Happy New Year!
>
> Jani Price
> Submissions Editor

Was this some sort of joke? Dan wondered. He reread the letter twice before dropping it on the bed, his entire body shaking in horror. *The New Yorker* rarely published poems by unknown writers, and Jani Price was famous for sending nasty one-line rejection letters like, "Nice try!" or "Sorry, Charlie." Dan studied the letterhead. It looked authentic. Then he read the letter again, his hands still shaking wildly at the thought of some stranger—let alone someone as famous in the literary world as Jani Price—reading his poem.

The more he thought about it, the more apparent it

became that the only person who could have sent the poem to the magazine in the first place was Vanessa. As if she hadn't done enough damage already. What the hell—no, what the *fuck* was she thinking?

Dan threw the letter down on his bed and pulled off his dirty shirt. First he was going to take a steaming hot shower and put on some clean clothes.

Finally!

Then he was going to head straight over to Brooklyn to chew Vanessa out. How dare she violate his work by sending it out to whomever she pleased without asking him first? Who'd she think she was, anyway? His shaven-headed, combat-boots-wearing fairy godmother?

How about the badass Good Witch of the East?

Ruby had finally retrieved the missing Sony digital camera and Vanessa was sitting at her computer, downloading the images of icicles from it and inserting them into her new film, right before some footage she'd taken of pigeons roosting inside a garbage truck. She had already deleted the footage of Nate and Jenny in the snow and had decided to put the whole thing behind her and focus on her new film instead. Beside the roosting pigeons a dirty, bald doll's head with a missing eye was sticking out of a burst garbage bag. It was awesome.

An instant message box appeared in the top right-hand corner of her computer screen and Vanessa clicked on it, hoping it was Dan. He might have heard from *The New Yorker* by now, and maybe he was IMing to say thank you because they'd decided to publish it and all was forgiven. But the address in the IM wasn't Dan's.

KM10001:   r u vanessa abrams, filmmaker?
Hairlesskat: maybe

KM10001: i'm looking for the person who filmed those kids in the park messing around. the camera work was not to be believed.
Hairlesskat: oh really? says who?
KM10001: Ken Mogul. i made Seahorse. maybe u've seen it. so am i talking to the right person?
Hairlesskat: yes.
KM10001: wow. so i'd really like to work with u. i'm finishing up a film now that i'm submitting at Cannes. r u interested?
Hairlesskat: i'm kind of still in high school. but yeah, i'm interested.
KM10001: cool. can i meet u somewhere? like later today? i'm in NYC btw.
Hairlesskat: i'm shooting in Central Park tonite @ 10pm or so. meet me there?
KM10001: excellent. i'd love to watch u work. see you then.
Hairlesskat: bye

Vanessa went back to editing her film knowing there was a big possibility that the person who had just IMed her was actually a group of Nate's preppy thug friends who were right now hacking a hole in the ice in the lake in Central Park so they could throw her into the freezing water and drown her because of the link that had been going around. Or maybe it really had been Ken Mogul, alternative filmmaker, one of her heroes. She laughed out loud. She was such a sucker for crank e-mails. But who knew? Anything was possible.

gossipgirl.net

topics ◀ previous   next ▶   post a question   reply

Disclaimer: All the real names of places, people, and events have been altered or abbreviated to protect the innocent. Namely, me.

hey people!

How to have the rockingest New Year's Eve ever

Two words of advice:

1) Stick with me. I know where the action is.

2) Kiss people. Tonight at midnight is the only time in the entire year when you have an open invitation to kiss completely random people without any explanation at all. So go for it!

Your e-mail

Dear Gossip Girl,
Okay, so I'm not usually a big gossip but I thought I'd tell you since I'm still down here in St. Barts. That boy **B** was hanging out with—**M**? Well, right after **B** left, he hooked up with this French girl who teaches water-skiing, and they've been spending a *lot* of time together.
—bean

Dear bean,
Thanks for the info. Sorry you're stuck there instead of here. BTW you should gossip more often. It makes your skin glow.
—GG

Sightings

A walking his Boxer down **Park Avenue**. Guess he's home from **St. Barts**, even if his friend **M** isn't. **Flow** hopping a plane from **LA** to New York's **Kennedy Airport** early this morning. Really?? **B** venturing outside to buy some **Frédéric Fekkai** extra-hold hairspray at **Zitomer**

Pharmacy on Madison. Looks like she's cooking up a wacky hairdo for the party tonight. Can't wait to see her. Can't wait to see you all!

The only party worth going to

If you haven't already gotten one of these, then you may as well leave town:

Don't be a loser.

Come celebrate New Year's Eve with me!

Theme: A Wild Night in Paradise

Where? The Ice Castle, West 19th Street

When? Sunday night, duh. 9 P.M. till . . .

Bring? Yourself and as many friends as you can fit in the elevator.

See you there!

—*Serena*

Our lives are better than the movies

If our lives were a bad teen movie, we'd invite the admissions officers of all the colleges we're applying to to come out with us and make sure they had a good enough time that they'd decide to let us in. But our lives are better than the movies, and we don't need to go to such extremes to get into college. *Right?*

Can't wait to see who's kissing who at midnight!

You know you love me,

gossip girl

j makes a break for it

Jenny had shaved, depilated, tweezed, exfoliated, and mois-
turized her entire body, polished her nails, blown out her
hair, and applied subtle makeup in gold and bronze tones
according to a chart she'd saved from *Allure* magazine. Then
she'd donned the thong and the same pair of black velvet
pants she'd been wearing that special day in the park, paired
with a tight black v-neck sweater with gold threads in it that
looked cheesy on the hanger but great on.

According to her, anyway.

Last of all, she put on the turquoise pendant Nate had given
her and a pair of pointy black high-heeled boots that were difficult
to walk in, but who cared? That was at six, and for the last two and
a half hours she'd tried to amuse herself by watching reruns of *The
Osbournes* and slowly demolishing an entire bag of Pepperidge
Farm cheddar-cheese-flavored goldfish, all the while keeping her
metallic blue cell phone cradled in her lap. But now it was already
eight-thirty on New Year's Eve and Nate still hadn't called.

Jenny had been so preoccupied with preparing her body
for the evening and waiting for Nate's call that she hadn't
really noticed what the rest of her family was doing. She
clicked off the TV and clomped up the hallway.

Dan's door was open a crack, and she pushed it open. The computer was off and no lit cigarettes burned in the ashtray.

"Dan?" she called out, but there was no answer.

She made an about-face and stomped down the hall to her father's office. The door stood open. Empty.

"Dad?" But again, no answer.

Traditionally on New Year's Eve Rufus went out with some of his cronies to an all-night poetry reading marathon in a café in Greenwich Village. It looked like he had already left.

Jenny pressed a few buttons on her cell phone and the phone instantly dialed Nate's number. The voicemail system answered, *again*.

"If you are trying to reach—," said the robotic female voice.

"Nate," Nate said in his own voice.

"Please press one and leave a message, or wait for the tone," the robotic female voice continued.

"It's me again," Jenny chirped, trying to sound upbeat. "I guess you got stuck in traffic or something. I think I'll just go to Serena's party now. Maybe I'll get the cab to stop by your house and buzz up. Anyway, hopefully I'll see you before midnight! Okay. Love you. 'Bye."

Jenny clicked off and went back into her room to get her bag and coat. So what if she wasn't officially ungrounded? Rufus and Dan had left her alone in the apartment.

What did they expect from a princess who'd been locked in her tower for too long?

Nate had considered not smoking at all until he got to the party because he knew Blair preferred it when he wasn't baked. But come on, it was New Year's Eve.

"'Ere," said Jeremy, passing Nate the enormous joint he had

just lit. Nate, Jeremy, and Anthony were huddled together near the Gandhi statue in Union Square. Nearby, someone was playing "Yesterday" on a recorder. "Take a big hit," Jeremy advised. "Then we'd better find that fucking party. It's like Antarctica out here."

Nate held the joint to his lips and sucked in, closing his eyes. There was nothing better than a good long hit on a freezing cold night. He handed the joint off to Charlie, holding the smoke in his lungs for a moment longer.

"What if the party sucks?" Charlie asked before taking a hit.

Nate remembered what Serena had said about Blair locking herself in her room all week so she could work on her Yale application. Whenever Blair spent a prolonged amount of time alone doing schoolwork, she was always extremely horny afterward.

"Dude," he said, blowing a cloud of smoke into the air near Gandhi's head. "Believe me, it won't suck."

n is still wearing b's heart on his sleeve

Leave it to Serena to raise the standard for New Year's Eve parties, or any party for that matter. Two minutes inside the Chelsea loft she'd rented for the extravaganza was long enough to make it clear this was definitely the best party anyone had ever been to. There were torches smoldering in the corners, and the dance floor was made of real green grass. The bartenders were wearing skimpy crocheted bikinis, and the DJ was some newly famous rocker from Iceland. At one end of the loft were three rooms with white leather couches and bathtubs in them, for those who needed some privacy or just wanted to take a bath. And there was a huge terrace with views of the city in three directions for when the fireworks started.

Blair hadn't slept for more than a few hours or been out of the house since she'd returned from St. Barts. She'd been running on espresso, adrenaline, cigarettes, and determination. Her screenplay was going to work, she could just feel it—it was going to get her into Yale!

But even the best auteurs need a little break.

She arrived at the party wearing a purple suede Dior microminiskirt, a black satin Chloé camisole, and black fishnet tights. Her hair was pulled up into a superhigh, superbouncy sixties ponytail and she was wearing false eyelashes and silver lipstick. On her feet were her newest pair of black suede Christian Louboutin four-inch-high ankle boots that her gay father had sent her from France as a Christmas present with a card that said, "Merry Christmas, Blair Bear. Warning: Do not go out unattended wearing these boots!" But Blair hadn't heeded his advice—she'd come alone.

It didn't take her long to find Serena. She was the only girl with pink streaks in her hair, dancing barefoot, and wearing a Missoni string bikini top, black velvet short shorts, and long, dangly diamond earrings. The DJ had cranked up the volume and the music was so loud the walls were shaking.

"My boobs hurt!" Serena shouted at Blair, still dancing.

"My brain hurts!" Blair shouted back. What she needed before she even thought about dancing or talking to anyone was a stiff drink.

Or three or four.

"I just saw Nate!" Serena shouted, pointing randomly into the crowd. "He was looking for you!"

Sure he was.

Blair ducked past Serena, pushing her way through the crowd toward the bar. She deserved to get drunk. She had almost finished her screenplay—all but the ending—and she was pretty sure it rocked. Plus it was New Year's fucking Eve, and if Nate wanted to talk to her, she wanted to have at least one drink in her first.

Kati and Isabel were standing by the bar waiting for their cosmos. "Hey, Blair," they cooed in unison.

"You're still tan," Isabel noted, poking her own pale arm in disgust.

They were both wearing long black halter dresses, exactly like the ones Blair and Serena had worn to the Black-and-White Ball.

"Serena said you were working on your Yale application," Kati said, slurping her cosmo. "We still have a whole month before our applications are due, you know."

Blair glared at the bartender for taking so long to take her order. "I just want it to be perfect."

"And I'm sure it will be," a familiar voice assured her.

Blair whirled around to find Nate—her leading man—standing right in front of her, wearing the moss green cashmere V-neck sweater she had given him last Easter. Before she'd wrapped it up and given it to him, she'd sewn a little gold heart pendant inside of one of the sleeves so that Nate would always be wearing her heart on his sleeve. She wondered if the heart was still there.

Kati and Isabel left them alone, slinking over to a group of girls who began whispering to one another.

"I heard she lost it to that Miles guy in St. Barts," said Tina Ford.

"That's why she came back early," added Rain Hoffstetter. "To get the morning-after pill from her gyno."

"Has anyone seen Flow?" Kati asked.

"Serena promised us he was going to come," whined Isabel.

Nicki Button shook her head knowingly. "I heard Flow broke up with Serena because he wants to stay clean and she's a total druggie."

"So, where's your little kindergartner?" Blair asked, pulling a Merit Ultra Light out of the pack in her purse and waiting for Nate to light it for her.

Nate grinned. It was a start. At least she was talking to him. "We broke up," he said simply.

Since *when?*

The bartender finally sauntered over in his skimpy crocheted bikini, and Nate slapped his hand on the bar. "Ketel One and tonic, and a Jack and Coke with lots of ice," he said, ordering for both of them.

Blair loved how Nate already knew exactly what she wanted without her having to say anything, but she pretended not to notice, smoking her cigarette and watching the dancers grind their asses into one another.

"So, how was your Christmas?" Nate asked, carefully handing her the overflowing vodka tonic.

Not the best conversation starter.

Blair took a large gulp and then a deep drag on her cigarette. "Shitty."

Nate could tell she didn't want to talk about it. "Never mind," he said. "Only six more months till graduation."

They looked at each other in wide-eyed horror.

"Six months," Blair repeated, taking another big gulp.

"That's way too long," Nate said, finishing her thought.

Blair almost ventured a smile. That was another thing she loved about Nate: He always knew exactly what she was thinking.

"It's crazy," Nate went on, encouraged by her hint of a smile. "Next year at this time, we're going to be hanging out with some new bunch of friends we met at college. People we don't even know exist yet."

Blair bit her cocktail straw, watching Serena bump butts with two dark-haired men in their twenties wearing matching navy blue sailor suits, who looked like twins. "I can't wait," she declared. "Once I get to Yale, I'm never coming back."

Nate smiled. He loved how Blair always just assumed she was going to Yale. "I'll have to come and visit you, then."

The vodka was going straight to Blair's head. She could see that Nate was trying to talk to her like nothing had happened, like he hadn't dumped her for a preschooler and spent the last month avoiding her entirely. It was kind of irritating, but it was also kind of wonderful, like the part in her screenplay where Audrey realized that Colin had been just as terrible to her as she'd been to him and she decided to love him even more for it. Blair took a deep breath and finished her drink. She'd forgotten how green Nate's eyes were.

Charlie Dern walked up to them and slapped Nate's palm. "Hey, welcome back, man. I saw your ass on that Web site. Nice work!"

Nice timing.

"Thanks, man," Nate responded, trying to be cool. "See you later," he added, clueing Charlie into the fact that he didn't want to discuss it.

Charlie took off and Blair put another cigarette into her mouth. "What'd he mean, nice work on what?"

Nate flicked open his Zippo and lit the cigarette for her. If Blair hadn't heard about him and Jennifer on that site everyone kept talking about, he definitely wanted it to stay that way. "Nothing," he answered.

A lock of sandy brown hair fell over his forehead and Blair brushed it away for him, letting herself smile up at him as he smiled back.

It almost felt like old times.

Almost.

a finds a distraction

A little after ten, Blair's long-lost stepbrother, Aaron, stepped off the elevator and into the loft in a cloud of herbal cigarette smoke, wearing one of his many black LEGALIZE HEMP T-shirts and looking surprisingly pale for having just spent a week in St. Barts.

Right away, his eyes cut across the heaving crowd of drinkers and smokers and sweaty dancers and homed in on Blair and Nate talking beside the bar, their eyes never straying from each other's faces. Aaron's heart slammed against the walls of his chest. Blair looked like a completely different person from the Blair in St. Barts. She was glowing.

He wanted to go up to her and apologize and try to explain his idiotic behavior in the villa, but then he thought better of it. This was a party, and they were all supposed to be having fun. He would just have to wait until tomorrow, if Blair wasn't too hungover.

Out on the dance floor, Serena spied Aaron's wild little dreadlocks and danced over to him, pink-streaked hair bouncing and silver-painted toes gleaming. She threw her arms around his neck and pressed her flushed cheek against his ear. "I'm so glad you came!" she said, sounding like she really meant it.

"Me too." Aaron grinned, thinking that maybe he meant it, too.

"Where's Miles? Didn't he come with you?"

Aaron shook his head. "He's still in St. Barts. He kind of met someone there."

Serena giggled. "Oh, did he?"

Aaron put his hands in his army pants pockets and glanced across the room at Blair and Nate again.

Serena followed his gaze. Why was Aaron always staring at Blair with that sad, sad look on his face? "It's so great to see them together again, isn't it?" she gushed breathlessly, hoping that he would agree.

Aaron forced himself to nod. Blair wasn't his to have, and she did look happy. "Yeah," he said. "It is."

Serena slipped her arm through his, leading him toward the dance floor. "Come on," she cried, "let's dance!"

She smelled like sandalwood and patchouli, and in her bare feet she was exactly the same height as Aaron was. *Wow*, Aaron realized as Serena raised her lithe, golden arms over her head and did a little spin, her pink-streaked hair flying out in all directions. *She really is gorgeous.*

Like everyone else in the entire world hadn't already noticed.

He might have looked a little pale when he arrived, but somebody was about to have a very happy New Year's Eve.

only in new york

Vanessa wasn't big on the idea of kissing a lot of drunk people she didn't like very much and shouting, "Happy New Year!" It was kind of her nightmare. So instead of going to Serena's party she'd packed up her camera equipment, put on lots of layers, and taken the subway to Central Park. Everyone who "belonged" would be at Serena's party, so why not see what the people who didn't belong were doing? It was only nineteen degrees outside, and the temperature was dropping. You couldn't get any more misfit than the people who were about to participate in the annual midnight run around the frozen park. It was the perfect denouement for her New York film essay.

She began to film people as they turned up for the race at the entrance to the park near the reservoir on East Eighty-ninth Street. It had begun to snow, so it was kind of a challenge to keep the lens clear and the lighting right, but the park looked incredibly pristine and beautiful with its thin coating of new snow, and the runners were all such total wackjobs. This was going to be even better than the doll's head in the garbage truck.

"Is the run something you do every year, or is this your first time?" Vanessa asked an emaciated man dressed only in denim cutoffs and basketball shoes with no socks. She zoomed in on his skinny, caved-in chest, checking for goose bumps, but scarily enough, she didn't see any.

"First time?" the man exclaimed, pulling his stringy gray hair back into a ponytail and grinning at her with tobacco-stained teeth. "Do I look like a virgin to you?"

Gross.

Vanessa was glad her face was hidden by the camera.

"All right," she said, backing away. "Good luck to you."

She backed right into a woman who must have been in her seventies wearing a mink coat, Chanel sneakers, and mink earmuffs, leading a white standard poodle that was also wearing a mink coat.

"Hey, who's this?" Vanessa crooned, squatting down to pet the dog.

"We love to run in the snow." The woman smiled gaily, her crinkly lips coated heavily with orangey pink lipstick. Her white hair was done up in a French twist, and her cheeks were thick with creamy orange rouge. "My children are all grown and my husband's off gambling in Nice, so Angel and I came here to amuse ourselves."

"Me too," Vanessa said, even though she obviously didn't have children or a husband or even a dog. She smiled conspiratorially at the woman. "It's a kick, isn't it?"

The woman was pulling something out of her green Hermès Kelly bag, and Vanessa zoomed in so she could see: Little red rubber booties.

"So he doesn't get snowballs in his paws," she explained, bending down to Velcro them on to the poodle's feet.

"And they're so stylish, too," Vanessa said.

Now she knew what people meant when they said, "Only in New York." Only in New York would you find a woman and her poodle in matching mink coats running in a midnight race with that weirdo in the cutoffs. And now she had a title for her film essay, too: *Only in New York*. It was brilliant, even if she did say so herself.

Boots on, Angel trotted around in a circle, showing them off. "Good boy!" Vanessa called, following him closely with the camera.

She was so enchanted by her subject she didn't even notice her hero, Ken Mogul, wander up and sit down on a nearby park bench to watch.

Dan had been looking for Vanessa for hours. First he'd gone to her apartment, which would have been the most obvious place to find her, but after buzzing the downstairs buzzer fourteen times and yelling up at the windows, he'd finally given up. Then he'd wandered over to the Five and Dime, the Williamsburg dive where Ruby's band, SugarDaddy, played. Ruby had been busy rehearsing with her band, but she'd told Dan Vanessa had mentioned something about filming crazy people in some park at midnight.

How helpful. As if every park in the entire city wasn't full of crazy people.

First Dan looked in Madison Square Park, where Vanessa had filmed her scene from *War and Peace*. But except for a few people walking their dogs and a man sleeping on a bench with a paper bag over his head, the park was quiet. Then he tried Washington Square Park, which was full of hipster skateboarders and NYU students lighting illegal firecrackers. Finally he walked uptown again to Central Park, wandering aimlessly through it and cursing Vanessa for not believing in cell phones. He circled the reservoir, watching the mini ice floes float around and bump into one another and wondering where the ducks had all gone. Then he noticed a crowd gathered below him near the Eighty-ninth Street entrance to the park. And working her way through the crowd, chatting with people as she squinted at them through her video camera, was a pale girl in a black overcoat, a black watch cap, and black combat boots.

Dan walked down the wide stone steps that led up to the reservoir and sat down on a park bench next to a guy in his thirties with curly red hair and freckly skin wearing an expensive-looking dark gray ski jacket with a fur-trimmed hood. The guy was sitting on his bare hands and appeared to be watching Vanessa intently.

"See how she gets up behind people before she goes up and talks to them?" the guy asked Dan, pointing at Vanessa. "It's like she's getting to know the part they don't even know about *themselves* yet."

Dan nodded. Who the hell was this guy, anyway?

"And I love the way she just melts into the background sometimes, keeping so still, just letting people do their thing. She's beautiful."

Dan turned and glared at the guy. He wanted to punch him.

The guy held out his hand. "Hey, I'm Ken Mogul, film-maker," he said. "Are you in the film business?"

Dan shook his hand briefly. "No," he said. His breath floated skyward in cold white puffs. "I'm a poet."

They both watched as Vanessa squatted down to let a poodle wearing a mink coat sniff her camera lens. Dan leaned forward. She was so graceful behind the camera and so at ease with what she was doing, it was hard to believe she would ever misuse her material. Maybe Jenny had been right not to blame Vanessa, he decided. Maybe she'd had nothing to do with posting that link. Somehow her work had just made it into the wrong hands.

"Ever had anything published?" Ken Mogul asked him.

"Not yet." Dan smiled to himself. "But I've got a poem coming out in *The New Yorker* next month," he added with pride.

what she wants is not what she has

It was almost eleven when Jenny turned up at Serena's party. Her overly friendly cabdriver had gotten stuck in traffic in Times Square—which everyone knows is the one place to avoid on New Year's Eve because it's crammed with drunken tourists and it's a complete nightmare. So Jenny got out and walked. She felt sort of mature and cool, out on her own at night, on her way to a party where she would finally see her boyfriend again, the love of her life.

When she stepped off the elevator and into the loft, Jenny unbuttoned her coat and handed it to the coat-check girl. Her stupendous boobs ballooned out of her black-and-gold knit V-neck top and into the room.

Hello, hello!

Several male party guests instantly recognized the petite curly-haired brunette from the Web link that had been such a hot item over break. They stopped what they were doing and began to applaud.

"Hey, come over here and show me your thong!" a random guy wearing an old-fashioned black top hat shouted drunkenly.

"Want to get inside my coat?" shouted another.

Jenny stood frozen in the doorway, clutching her purse, and feeling very much like Clara in the *Nutcracker* when she's surrounded by the gang of evil mice. Her eyes searched the room looking desperately for Nate.

Where, oh, where was her Nutcracker Prince?

Across the room, standing next to the bar, a boy with wavy golden brown hair and a girl with long dark hair that hung down the middle of her back were talking to each other with their faces so close together, they might as well have been kissing. They were looking at each other in exactly the way Jenny always wanted to be looked at, like they'd forgotten they were at a party full of people, too distracted by love.

The boys were still clapping and hooting at Jenny when the golden-haired boy and the brown-haired girl turned their heads to look.

Hello, hello *again!*

And in that instant, Jenny *knew.*

Nate had never been in love with her, because he'd never stopped being in love with Blair. And because he had lied and pretended he loved her, he wasn't even a good boyfriend, like Vanessa and Dan had said he was. Nate was no Nutcracker Prince. He was just another rotten *mouse.*

"Nate," Jenny gasped, her voice catching in her throat. She wobbled up to where he and Blair were standing by the bar, yanked the turquoise pendant from her neck, and threw it at him as hard as she could.

"Jennifer, I'm sorry—," Nate started to sputter, but his eyes didn't look very sorry and Jenny wasn't interested. Blair was glaring at her, but that didn't bother her, either.

"Fuck you," she whispered as hot tears began to roll down her cheeks. Then she turned away to find the bathroom so she could splash cold water on her face and leave the party with some dignity.

Nate bent down and stuffed the turquoise pendant into his pocket. He looked tired and clumsy. Blair put another cigarette between her lips and struck a match against the flint, trying to light it. She kept striking it without any luck and finally let the match drop with an exasperated sigh.

Nate opened his Zippo and held it out to her, but Blair ignored him. "What's wrong?" he asked, although he was pretty sure he knew.

Blair narrowed her eyes at him, the unlit cigarette still hanging from her mouth. He wasn't her leading man. He was a has-been. And there were so many promising young stars out there—what did she need him for? "You're another reason I can't wait to go to college."

"I just want to light your cigarette," Nate responded lamely.

"Okay." Nate lit the cigarette and Blair inhaled deeply. Then she blew a stream of smoke into his face. "But now you can fuck off."

Nate frowned and closed the Zippo, extinguishing the flame. Blair was always overreacting. Around them people began to chant, "Ten! Nine! Eight!"

"Blair?" Nate took a step forward. All they had to do was kiss and make up and everything would go back to normal again. Just like old times.

But Blair was already gone, dropping her burning cigarette at Nate's feet, her high brown ponytail swishing between her shoulder blades as she headed for the sliding glass doors leading out to the deck. It was almost midnight, and she had better things to do than kiss another loser.

s gets serenaded

Serena had been dancing so hard, she felt like she'd been running a marathon. Her mouth was dry, her legs ached, and her arms hung loosely at her sides. Someone had spilled their drink in her hair, but she didn't care. There was a very cute butt grooving very close to her own butt, and the butt was dressed in green army pants and belonged to a very cute boy with short, dark dreadlocks.

"Seven! Six! Five!"

Aaron grabbed Serena's hand. "Let's go outside!" he yelled, pulling her across the room toward the sliding glass doors.

"Serena!" a voice called, stopping them in their tracks.

Serena turned around, her blue eyes wide with disbelief. It was Flow, stepping off the elevator wearing a tan suede coat and carrying his guitar case. There were circles under his eyes and his curly black hair was a little flat on one side from the long plane ride from LA, but he was still gorgeous. The girls at the party all stopped and stared, and so did most of the guys.

"Hi." Serena flashed him an awkward smile.

Flow breathed her in like a breath of fresh air. In her string bikini top, short shorts, and bare feet, she looked like the goddess of his wildest dreams. He knelt down and unsnapped his guitar case. "I wrote a song for you on the way out here."

Serena dropped Aaron's hand and folded her arms across her chest. She didn't want to be rude, but at what point was Flow going to just *give it up and go home?*

Beside her Aaron slouched with his hands in his pockets. He didn't mind hearing what Flow had to play. Neither did anyone else in the room.

"It's called 'My Kandy Girl,'" Flow murmured quietly. He slung his guitar strap over his shoulder, strummed a few chords, and then squeezed his eyes shut as he began to sing.

> *You stole my heart, now I'm paying the fine*
> *You cleaned me out, left me high and dry*
> *My love is like chocolate; it melts in your hand*
> *If only you'd taste it, then you'd understand*

Ick. But remember, he had that *face.*

It was probably the worst song ever written, but the party guests still swarmed around Flow, mesmerized by the music and his hunky good looks. The girls were all hoping he'd notice them and improvise a song for them on the spot, and the guys were all thinking that if they hung out with Flow, they were sure to get lucky tonight.

Serena was tempted to toss a dollar into Flow's guitar case, but she was probably already breaking his heart—she didn't have to insult him on top of it.

"Come on," she whispered to Aaron, backing into the crowd and tugging on his hand. "Let's go outside."

Blair wasn't surprised when Chuck Bass found her standing out on the deck, furiously eating olives, smoking cigarettes, gulping Veuve Clicquot, and freezing her ass off. It was just before midnight, and knowing Chuck, he was looking for someone to give him a blow job while the fireworks went off.

"Happy New Year, Blair." Chuck walked right up and kissed her on the lips. There was an olive pit in her mouth, but he didn't seem to mind.

Blair pulled away and spat the pit on the ground. "It better be."

Chuck put his arm around her and then slowly slid his hand down her back and over her ass. "You know what's the best way to ring in the new year?"

She pulled away and pointed through the glass doors to where Kati and Isabel were standing on a little table holding each other's hands and counting down the new year.

"Those two have always been totally in love with you," Blair declared, trying to keep a straight face. "If you want to 'ring in the new year' with someone, why don't you ask them?"

Chuck grinned at her. "Really?"

She nodded. "Go ahead, I'm—" But before she could even finish her sentence, Chuck ducked back inside and grabbed the two girls in a group hug.

"Four! Three! Two!"

v and *d* have their own display

At eleven forty-five, the runners had started their slow course around the park. Vanessa jogged alongside them with her video camera, trying to capture the mixture of determination, pain, and elation on their faces. They were outside, running, and it was freezing! It was the end of an old year and the beginning of a new one—maybe even the beginning of a new era!

Even though they were moving so slowly she could have easily kept up with them, Vanessa had left her bag of camera equipment behind in the snow and her combat boots were giving her blisters, so she decided to head back to the starting point, figuring she'd catch up with them at the finish.

Dan and Ken Mogul were still waiting for her on the bench.

"I've been nominated for a few things," Ken was saying. "But I never won anything. Maybe working with Vanessa will change that." He had kept up a running monologue ever since Dan sat down beside him.

Dan didn't mind. His notebook was open on his lap and he was staring fixedly at the halo of light cast by a streetlamp in the snow, searching for the exact words to describe the way the snowflakes were drifting through the light, so slowly they didn't seem to be falling so much as floating.

All of a sudden Vanessa stepped into the halo of light, her cheeks red from running and her huge brown eyes shining. She smiled at the ridiculous sight of Dan and some older guy in a fancy ski parka sitting together on a park bench, a half inch of fresh snow dusting their shoulders. Dan's soulful brown eyes gazed up at her from underneath his white knit cap. He didn't look mad. God, was she glad to see him.

"How long have you been sitting there?"

The guy in the ski parka stood up. "Long enough to see that you're definitely the next great thing to happen to film."

Vanessa laughed again. Was this guy for real?

He walked over and handed her his card. *Ken Mogul, filmmaker*, the card read. "I'm heading down to Brazil to shoot an exposé on some kid prostitutes in Rio," Ken explained. "But I hope you'll call me so we can set something up. I could really use you."

Vanessa walked over to her camera bag and dumped her camera into it. She had always admired Ken Mogul's work, but she wasn't so sure she wanted to be "used" by some director, no matter how famous he was. She wanted to make it on her own.

"Will you call me?" Ken persisted.

"Excuse me," she heard Dan say quietly behind them.

Ken turned around. "This guy's been waiting to talk to you almost as long as I have. Who are you, anyway, man?"

Dan stood up, letting his notebook fall into the snow. He walked over to Vanessa, grabbed her, and wrapped her in his arms. "Her boyfriend," he told Ken Mogul over her shoulder. And then he kissed her as hard as he could, afraid that if he did it too meekly she wouldn't take him seriously. He was her boyfriend, goddammit! And he was mad at her, and proud of her, and proud of himself for kissing her and ending this madness once and for all.

Vanessa kissed him back just as hard. Screw Ken Mogul, filmmaker. The film she was making was much cooler than any film he'd ever made. Besides, she didn't feel like talking about her career right now, anyway. She was too busy kissing Dan, her boyfriend.

As they kissed, fireworks began to light up the sky overhead. It was the sort of cliché that could ruin a film or poem, but this was way better than a film and way better than a poem. It was the real thing.

j disses famous rock star

On the last note of the song, Flow opened his eyes to find Serena gone. The clock struck midnight and everyone began hugging and kissing and blowing their paper party horns, ignoring him completely, which was definitely a first for him.

A few people had thrown hundred-dollar bills into his guitar case just for the hell of it. He fished them out and threw them on the floor before settling his guitar back inside and snapping the case closed. Then he spun around to grab the elevator just as the doors were closing, wedging his case in between the doors until they rolled open again.

A short, curly-haired girl with a remarkably large chest was leaning against the back wall of the elevator.

"Hey." Flow smiled his famous shy-boy grin as he stepped inside.

The girl didn't say anything. She looked like she'd been crying.

"Are you headed downtown?" Flow asked. "I have a car waiting outside. Maybe I could buy you a drink or something."

Jenny kept her eyes on the floor. Flow, Nate, they were all

the same. Just because he was famous and hot didn't mean she had to talk to him, did it?

No, it most certainly did not.

The elevator doors opened. "Get lost," she replied.

She passed through the building's revolving glass door and stepped out onto the sidewalk to hail a cab. It was New Year's Eve and the city was one big party, but Jenny was going home to follow her dad's advice for once and curl up in bed with a good book.

As soon as Serena and Aaron made it outside, fireworks exploded in the sky all around them. It was freezing, and there were only a few people out on the deck. Everyone else was inside pouring champagne over one another's heads and dancing their butts off as the DJ cranked the music up even louder than before.

As she looked out at the psychedelic landscape, Serena had that feeling again—the one she loved—when she wasn't quite sure what would happen next, but she knew it would be something good. Maybe even the best thing yet.

"Look." She pointed as the sparks from a huge blue firework began to whiz around the sky and then explode in their own mini fireworks display over the East River.

Aaron lit an herbal cigarette. He was only wearing a T-shirt, but he didn't feel cold. "I didn't used to like fireworks," he said, blowing smoke into the air. "I thought they were loud, bad for the environment, and a waste of money."

"But you like them now, right?" Serena asked, turning to look at him. She had borrowed someone's sheepskin coat from off a chair but her feet were still bare, and she and Aaron really were exactly the same height.

Aaron nodded. "I love them."

"Me too," Serena breathed. Her whole body was shaking, and she wasn't sure if it was from the cold or because they were about to kiss.

Aaron took her hand. "Are you warm enough?"

"Yes."

His dark red lips curved up at the corners. "Let's not kiss until the fireworks are over, okay?"

"Okay," Serena said, surprised. And there was nothing she liked better than being surprised. Out over Times Square a new crescendo of fireworks had just begun. "Although I may not be able to wait."

Now that the hummingbird had found a flower it wanted to hang out on for a while, all it wanted to do was land.

"Why don't you just kiss now? You can always kiss some more later," a girl said behind them.

It was Blair, standing only a few feet away, wrapped in her sky blue Marc Jacobs coat but still shivering from the cold.

"Happy New Year." She walked over and kissed Aaron on the cheek.

Aaron hugged her. A nice, normal, brotherly hug. "Happy New Year, Sis."

Blair broke away from him to hug Serena.

"Happy New Year!" the two girls squealed, pressing their faces into each other's hair. It was crazy to think that for part of the year they'd wanted to kill each other. Now they didn't know what they'd do without each other.

"Okay." Blair pulled away. "Now you two can kiss."

Leaving them to decide whether to go ahead and kiss right away or not, she walked to the end of the deck and looked out over the Hudson River and New York Harbor. She watched as the fireworks exploded over the Statue of Liberty and plunged into the deep black water.

The second to last scene in her screenplay ended with a kiss. Now all she had left to write was the final scene, the ending.

It wasn't really going to end, she decided now. Not with any sort of finality. The best stories never did. Maybe she'd just cut to the next morning. Audrey would have a funny little exchange with the deli guy she bought her coffee from. Then she would laugh to herself, take a sip of her coffee, and walk out the door and into the street, leaving everybody guessing.

Disclaimer: All the real names of places, people, and events have been altered or abbreviated to protect the innocent. Namely, me.

hey people!

Okay, so I definitely got my wish about a life-changing New Year's Eve. I think just about everyone who went to that insanely amazing party did. I mean, how many of you actually believed **Flow** would show up? Too bad for him, the party got even better *after* he left.

Your e-mail

 Hey GG,
I heard that whole party was paid for with **S**'s drug money. I didn't go, but how else would she have gotten that DJ?
—underworld

 Dear underworld,
S has enough cash not to need drug money to throw a kick-ass party. Plus, if you weren't there, why are you even talking about it?
—GG

 Dear GG,
I think I danced with you on New Year's Eve. Do you have long blond hair and a great bod?
—CliffS

 Hello CliffS,
Maybe. That's all I'm saying.
—GG

Sightings

Dawn, New Year's Day: **C** asleep with his arms around **K** and **I** on a sofa in the **Tribeca Star Hotel** lobby. Guess they never even made it up to his family's suite. **N** doing bong hits with his friends in **Union Square Park**. No better way to finish the evening than the way you started it. **V** and **D** holding hands in the **Strand**. Only those two could get turned on by a bookstore. **S** and **A** eating breakfast at **Florent**, looking tired but very happy. **B** buying a huge cup of coffee in a **Madison Avenue** deli before hurrying into her building. And **J** burning paintings in a metal trash can on **West End Avenue** while trying to teach herself how to smoke. Now that she's jaded, she has to look the part.

Some lingering questions

Will **B** ever lose it? And if so, *with whom?*

Will **N** redeem himself, even though we'll still love him if he doesn't?

Will **S** settle down and stick with **A** for longer than a day?

Will **D** be ready to do it with **V** now that he's a published author?

Will **J** find true love?

Will any of us get over our hangovers in time to finish our college applications?

More importantly, will any of us get in anywhere?

Not that I'm too worried. Next semester is going to be one party after another, and I'm planning to enjoy myself.

Until next time.

You know you love me,

gossip girl

Scandal. Intrigue. Deception.
What else are friends for?

Be sure to read the first two Gossip Girl novels,
Gossip Girl and *You Know You Love Me*.

And keep your eye out for the fourth
book in the Gossip Girl series, coming
September 2003